June 20, 1998

To Sidney King

Best Wishes

Thomas R. G. Rice

THUNDER

ON THE

WESTERN FRONT

by

Thomas Russell G. Rice

1998

Copyright © 1998 Thomas Russell G. Rice. Printed and bound in the United States of America. All rights reserved. No part of this book may be reproduced or transmitted in any form or by any means, electronic or mechanical, including photocopying, recording, or by an information storage and retrieval system, except by a reviewer who may quote brief passages in a review to be printed in a magazine or newspaper_ without permission in writing from the publisher. Fro information, please contact Thomas Russell G. Rice, P.O. Box 1100, Dunnsville, VA 22454.

Although the author and publisher have made every effort to ensure the accuracy and completeness of information contained in this book, we assume no responsibility for errors, inaccuracies, omissions, or any inconsistency herein. Any slights of people, places, or organizations are unintentional.

All names are fictitious with the exception of the American, British and German generals and field marshals, Captain Ignasio Garcia, and other dignitaries mentioned.

This is a novel which contains minimal fiction and is based on a true story.

First Printing 1998

ISBN 1-889074-06-3

DEDICATION

Dedicated to my wife, Esther Wilhelm Rice, who inspired me to write this book.
My mother, Louise Bray Rice, deceased,
My brothers who are also deceased:
Lieutenant William G. Rice, United States Navy
Joseph F. Rice, Infantry United States Army
Charles W. Rice, Sr., War Historian;
and last, but not least,
Captain Ignasio Garcia, United Sates Army

My sincere thanks to David Wallace, Editorial Assistant, Pocahontas Press, who read my manuscript, and gave me unlimited support during the preparation of this entire book.

CONTENTS

Chapter		Page
1	In the Beginning - A Perilous Odyssey	1
2	A Venture Into An Ancient Land	5
3	Invasion of a Strategic Island	7
4	Victory, and Return to England	12
5	A New Assignment	15
6	Let the War Games Begin	23
7	Arrival in France and Drive Into History	34
8	The Battle of the Bulge	44
9	Through the Siegfried Line to the Rhine	54
10	From Battle Casualty and Back to Combat	61
11	Across the Rhine, Central Europe and Victory	71
12	Postwar Cry of the Werewolf	76
13	To Valenciennes	82
14	Back to the Good Old United States of America	88

Chapter 1
In the Beginning - A Perilous Odyssey

As a volunteer draftee in the Army of the United States on January 20, 1943 (my birthday), I was inducted at Camp Lee, Virginia. From Camp Lee I was sent to Camp Pickett, Virginia, and received my basic training as a battlefield medical aide man. I had applied for training in the armored forces, but it didn't work out that way, which was not surprising.

After eleven weeks of basic training, I was sent to a staging area in Pennsylvania, Camp Shenango. Two weeks later found me in Camp Shanks, New York, which turned out to be my port of embarkation. While there I enjoyed the exotic night life in New York City for the first time. I even got to see Jack Dempsey in uniform at his famous club.

In approximately a week's time, the North African Campaign was about over, so the rumor that we would be sent there went sour. After a two-day restriction, due to a First Lieutenant in my group telling us too much, we were taken by train to Pier 56 in New York where we boarded the HMS *Queen Mary*. The HMS *Queen Mary* sailed the following day with approximately 20,000 troops bound for the British Isles. The Company I was assigned to was Casual Company F, so being a group of this sort, we could be designated most any place. Our Company was very lucky aboard this overcrowded vessel, as it was assigned to the galley and mess as KPs for the entire voyage of six days from New York to Gourock, Scotland, on the River Clyde. On the day of our arrival in Gourock, the Lieutenant informed our Company that we would be the last troops to depart the *Queen Mary*. Five days later, after cleaning up all the damn mess left by thousands of troops, our Casual Company boarded a landing craft, then transferred to a troop train for an overnight trip to a replacement center near Birmingham, England.

Upon arrival at this replacement center, our group was lectured by a tough Colonel, while standing in pouring rain for one solid hour at attention! When dismissed, all of our Casual Company were given a mattress cover which was stuffed with hay, then spread on the wet ground under leaking tents where the duration of our short stay was spent.

The following morning, a sparse breakfast of oatmeal, powdered eggs, and coffee, all cold, was served to us. Our group, trained as field aide men, was called out for special assignment.

Along with a contingent of infantry trainees, we were marched with full field equipment in a column of twos for two miles in pouring rain to a waiting troop train. As soon as our Company had boarded, each soldier with a full field pack and two duffle bags, the train moved out so quickly that some of us barely got our bags on board. The rest of the day and on through the darkness, this train traversed the English countryside, arriving at the seaport of Plymouth by first light at 0400 on a very dreary morning.

Our Company, along with many other American and British troops, upon reaching dockside were marched aboard a very large freighter, painted haze gray and camouflaged to the utmost.

Most of the troops were quartered between decks around the cargo holds, but our Casual Company was assigned to the main deck, as we would be permanent KPs for the entire voyage.

When I had the chance, I asked one of the British seamen, "Mate, just where in the hell are we bound anyway?" His answer was, "Matey, you are bloody well going to North Africa, if this domm hulk can survive 'Jerry's' U-boat torpedoes!" So I answered, "but the war is over in North Africa, so what the hell?" He then replies, "O I know Yank, but it ain't over in Sicily and Italy, and damn soon that's where the bloody 'ell you will be going!" "Thanks, mate," I spoke out as I went on about my business of finding a spot to rest before time to dish out the chow.

Our Casual Company was commanded by Captain Angus MacDaniel, who was one of the finest and most understanding officers in the Army of the United States, and that also went for the First Lieutenant, who was second in command. Most of our group were well-trained battlefield medics out of Camp Pickett, Virginia, and were very proud to be heading into future combat and history!

This was a long, lonely, and treacherous voyage aboard the *Albatross*, traversing the English Channel from Plymouth on through the outer fringes of the Bay of Biscay, well off the coast of the Iberian Peninsula to the Straits of Gibraltar, on a wartime zig-zag course.

On day twelve out of Plymouth, England, the *Albatross* was attacked by a Nazi U-boat which surfaced west of Cape St. Vincent. Activating the deck gun, the submarine fired two projectiles which exploded close by our starboard bow! The U-boat Captain (speaking guttural English) called out on his megaphone, "abandon ship as best you can with lifeboats und life rafts available, und I vill allow you one-half hour before I send your ship to der bottom!" After that threat of annihilation, our ship's Captain was mad as hell, as he picked up his megaphone on the bridge wing and yelled out, "if you bloody Jerry's had a damn torpedo left, you would have sunk us without warning. Now we will see whose bloomin' arse gets blown out of the water!" All at once, a six-inch gun was raised to deck level by an elevator and British gunners fired point blank at the surfaced U-boat making a direct hit on the afterdeck. Well, those Krauts abandoned the deck gun, clambered down the open port of the Conning Tower, then submerged, just as the British gunners made several more geysers of water appear close-by the hull of the disappearing U-boat. "That should teach those bloody Nazis a damn good lesson to not underestimate the fighting spirit of the British," the Captain called out! He then gave the order, "gunners, standby until further orders!" All during this ordeal, my buddy, Tommy Smith, and I were watching from a concealed position behind some deck machinery. The rest of our group, along with other troops were standing by with life jackets, just as all aboard were, to follow any emergency orders given. After an hour had passed, with the ship moving at full ahead off the west coast of Spain, the big gun disappeared below decks, as the trap door closed the deck opening behind it.

 The weather had been bad, and the sea rough, all the way from Plymouth, England, to Cape St. Vincent, Portugal, and visibility had been very limited during this voyage. After the U-boat encounter, the sea began to smooth out in this area of the Atlantic, and skies began to open up off Spain's west coast, onward to the Straits of Gibraltar.

 Passing through the timeless Straits and on between the famous Pillars of Hercules on day fourteen, brought our position close-by the gigantic Rock of Gibraltar, and what a wonderful sight it was! At Gibraltar, our vessel was joined by a British destroyer which for the next three days, escorted us through the turquoise blue Mediterranean Sea to the port of Tunis, Tunisia. During this time, off the coast of Algeria, we were harassed by three Nazi "Stuka" dive bombers, but before they could zero in this target, one was shot down and the other two were deterred by the destroyers' antiaircraft guns.

Chapter 2
A Venture Into An Ancient Land

Debarking in Tunis, our Casual Company was marched to a line of waiting trucks and moved to a tent area set up outside the city; darkness was upon us as we settled in for the night, after a meal of fried Spam, dehydrated potatoes, and peas. The coffee was like motor oil, but hot enough to bring warmth and stimulation to the bodies of a very tired bunch of soldiers!

After pulling guard duty for half of the night, I had only slept for about four hours when awakened by Smith, "Buzz," (which was my nickname) he said, "let's try for a pass, and see the sights in the old city of Tunis. Maybe we can open up a keg of nails!" "Tommy," I answered, "we could be opened up ourselves if we are not careful, especially in the dark, narrow streets of the old Medina, where the real culprits operate. Orders are out that no wristwatches are to be worn on pass, as some of these natives have gone so far as to amputate the hand in order to get at them."

The war had passed through this area only a month ago, and it was very unsettled. Field Marshal Montgomery's Eighth Army had come in from the east, and General George S. Patton's Second Corps from the west, catching Field Marshal Irwin Rommel's "Afrika Korps" in a pincer movement. The last big battle of Kesserine Pass had been won by the Allies, and thousands of German troops had been pushed, cornered and trapped along the Mediterranean coast at Bizerte, Tunisia. Even though the remnants of the crack Nazi "Afrika Korps" were trapped at Bizerte, it's commander, Field Marshal Rommel (The Desert Fox) had somehow eluded his conquerors in a daring escape! Elusive as his nickname, Rommel had disappeared as if by magic. Most likely he had been picked up during hours of darkness by a Nazi submarine, while the confusion was at its height, in this last stand on the African continent. Field Marshal Montgomery, General Patton, as well as all allied commanders and troops were overly disappointed at Rommel's absence in Bizerte. The "Desert Fox" was cornered, but still managed to elude his hunters, to perhaps once more become a hunter, instead of the hunted. Hitler will most probably use him in the future to try and stem the tide of the great invasion when it does take place in western Europe, in the not too distant future, most probably in the Normandie Provence of France.

Getting back to Tommy's and my plans to venture into Tunis, we departed by truck, along with four other soldiers, because there is much more safety in numbers, as one ventures into the old Medina of North Africa. We all enjoyed the old market places and the dark, narrow streets of the old Casbah with the hawking salesmen, robed natives, and beggars. Also, we did thoroughly enjoy the wild French Cafe we stumbled onto with its flowing wine and pretty French-Arabian mademoiselles. Two of these dark-haired beauties latched onto Tommy and me, so we spent the entire evening in their company. After escorting these beauties home and joining them in more wine, music, and dance, Tommy and I departed their company just before midnight. On our way back to meet the other guys, we became hopelessly lost in a real dangerous section of this old Medina. Thanks to the gracious God that we ran smack into a contingent of Military Police who saw us safely to our destination!

Detailed for guard duty for the next several days during hours of darkness, Tommy and I did get to see more of this ancient city of Tunis during daylight hours. The architecture of Tunis was a real fantasy right out of the Arabian nights, and the timeless mosques with their praying towers reaching into the sky were dire wonders in all their splendor!

After a week in this tent area, our medical group, along with all equipment, plus medication and a supply of DDT, relocated in the Bizerte area. It was an overnight move by trucks, and once set up there, we were assigned to duties of processing and delousing the remnants of Rommel's "Afrika Korps!" Literally thousands of these German prisoners were processed and designated for POW camps in the United States and Britain. Most were Nazis and arrogant as hell, but we finally got them squared away, before our time to get ready for the ordeal ahead.

Chapter 3
Invasion of a Strategic Island

After July 1, 1943, our field medical aide men were attached to the amphibious forces that would take part in the invasion of Sicily. We knew the invasion would take place on this island, but didn't know where or when we would hit it! I had an older brother, who was assigned to an infantry division somewhere close-by in North Africa, but there was no way to look him up, due to much secrecy in operations during these perilous times.

Assigned to a regiment of a spearheading infantry division of the Seventh Army, the LSTs and LCIs headed out into the Mediterranean from Bizerte. On July 10, 1943, we hit the invasion beach at Gela, Sicily, amid a hail of 88 mm artillery, machine gun, and rifle fire. Being under the command of General George S. Patton, it was no surprise to see him on the invasion beach raising hell, while directing a group of Sherman tanks into action under intense enemy fire!

There were many casualties that first day, and this group of field medics used beaucoup tourniquets, bandages, morphine surets, and sulfadiazine. The stretcher bearers were also damn busy taking wounded to the aid station that had been set up. Being a battlefield medic is no picnic with only a Red Cross band on the arm and a red cross on the helmet, to protect you from an enemy who is firing at anything that moves. Several of our medics were hit the first day, some with rifle, and machine gun fire, and others with shrapnel. It seems that the enemy pays not much attention to the rules set up by the Geneva Convention, so we take this into consideration as we brave the ruthless fire upon the unarmed, as well as the armed, in this hell of battle. This invasion force had support fire from American and British warships firing projectiles into the enemy's defenses, as well as much allied air support, but the advancing tanks and infantry are the battle winners! Even though our fighter planes dominated the air over the invasion area, the Nazi Luftwaffe let their presence of ME109s, Ju88s and Stuka dive bombers be known from time to time, even though they were outnumbered. Off Gela, an American ammunition ship received a direct hit by a Stuka dive bomber which lit up the universe.

There really is no glory in battle, as war is as close to hell as one can imagine. Real glory only comes with all out victory!

Getting back to basics, our infantry and tanks advanced slowly from the invasion beaches to the higher grounds under intense enemy resistance (and mounting casualties really kept the medics busy!). One of our crack airborne divisions was making quite a name for itself also on this strategic island, as was also Field Marshall Montgomery, and his British forces (who were heading eastward toward Catania). This was entirely an Anglo-American operation, and from all indications it would definitely prove a success, even though there was a certain amount of jealousy between commanders!

Germany had some well battle-seasoned Wehrmacht troops in Sicily, along with crack SS Panzer units commanded by Field Marshal Kesselring, but their supplies were just about cut off, and they were no match for the superiority of our allied forces. Also we had the cooperation of most of the Italians, as they didn't want to see mass destruction of their beautiful island.

Once our armored and infantry began the big drive toward the northwest, backed up by artillery and air support, Palermo and all surrounding areas were conquered in the very short time period of twelve days. The Italian people were very friendly as they welcomed us to their cities, as well as their homes. The tide in the Mediterranean theatre had definitely turned, as without supplies, the German Wehrmacht were surrendering by the hundreds. Of course, there were many hard-line SS to deal with, but this was expected. After all casualties were given first aid and brought into the field hospital set up in the Palermo area, and all POWs had been processed, some of us took advantage of this short lull before the next move.

I hadn't seen my buddy, Smith, for several days, but all at once he showed up in the emergency section of the field hospital assisting the stretcher bearers with a wounded infantryman. "Buzz," he said, "I know you have been through as much hell as I have for the last two weeks, and it's time we got a break! Let's do some exploring in Palermo this evening!" "Fine with me," I answered, "if it's OK with 'Doc' here." Lieutenant Gray, the officer in charge, looked my way saying, "Buzz, get the hell out of here and have a ball tonight, as we don't know what tomorrow may have in store for us!" Smith and I then took off on foot, into the residential section of this seaport city where the streets were well patrolled by our infantry soldiers. In a short while we came upon two very pretty signorinas sitting on the front steps of a residence. As we walked up, they smiled, and the oldest one said, "Welcome to Palermo, Americans. Welcome to our home. Mama Mia is fix very nice spaghetti, and we have vino rosa for you!" Well, that was an invitation that Smith and I accepted wholeheartedly! "Very well, signorina," I answered, as they led us into their very clean modest home which smelled of good Italian cooking. I was very surprised at their almost fluent English, but learned later that they had taken it in school, and also they had family members living in the United States of America.

Mama Mia had prepared a wonderful Italian dinner which included spaghetti for the main course, along with homemade Italian bread and unlimited vino rosa. A curfew was in effect, so after partaking of this fine meal, nobody ventured outside the home. "Mama Mia say you stay in home tonight, and we make you very happy," said the oldest sister to us. "We have music radio, we dance, we drink vino rosa and have good times, war finish for now!" That is exactly what we did, and the following morning Smith and I departed, after a breakfast of freshly baked bread, hot coffee, and a big hug and kiss from the signorinas, also a bear hug from big Mama Mia!

After a couple of more days in Palermo, where the friendly Sicilians had passed out fruit, unlimited vino (and just about passed the city's keys) to the allied forces of Patton's Seventh Army, orders came in to head for Messina. On July 22, 1943, our Seventh Army, having already sliced this island in half, began pushing across the rough terrain of northern Sicily toward Messina, 200 miles to the east, on the narrow Straits of Messina which separates Sicily from Italy. This was really rough going, as this mountainous and rocky terrain was almost as bad to contend with as was the enemy. Without the primary donkey to carry supplies, we would all be up the creek without paddles! My buddy Smith remarked to me one day as we were taking the ancient city of Troina, "Buzz, if I ever make it out of this island of rocks and crags alive, I never want to see nothing but level land and no more donkeys ever!" "I'm sick of it too, Smith," I answered, "but just wait until we invade Italy. You ain't seen nothing yet!" "Maybe not," he replied, "but it's hell!"

The Italian army had just about moved out of the picture, as those who hadn't surrendered had changed to civilian clothes and disappeared into the surrounding hills. These friendly Sicilians were definitely on our side, and each town and village turned out to welcome us with open arms, along with delicious fruit and vino. The Germans were outnumbered, but they were not giving up their positions without a fight, and their eternal 88 mm projectiles pounded our positions much of the time. There were many casualties to contend with as our infantry, backed up with limited tanks and artillery (due to the primitive roads) fought gallantly across the north-central area of Sicily, linking up with the British south of Mount Etna. The German army in retreat was leaving mass destruction in their wake, as they blasted bridges along the narrow primitive roads. However, our engineers did wonders as they bridged these deep gaps (temporarily) in record time during our continuous pursuit of the retreating enemy!

Messina was captured on August 17, 1943. The entire island of Sicily was now in allied hands. However, the bad news was that literally thousands of German troops had eluded air and naval patrols, and managed to get across the narrow Straits of Messina into mainland Italy. Those enemy soldiers who hadn't escaped, put up a last stand fight, but surrendered after learning that they were in a hopeless situation.

Mussolini had been stripped of his power by King Victor Emmanuel as of July 24, 1943, so now Field Marshal Kesselring and his Wehrmacht were on their own, without the cooperation of the Italian army!

With the battle of Sicily over, and victory was ours, just about all of these American GI Joes and British Tommies were celebrating with the happy Sicilians. The night of August 17th on into the following day, vino rosa was flowing like water, as was dancing in the streets with pretty signorinas, to music that only these natives could make happen! Smith and I made sure all of the battle casualties were taken care of in our area, before we joined in this fantastic victory celebration!

On the morning of August 18th, my buddy Tommy Smith said to me, "Buzz, look at that land over there across the Straits, the sparse mountain and ridges look so very foreboding!" "Smith," I answered, "that land over there is the beginning of the 'boot' of Italy, and nothing can penetrate those ridges short of men and donkeys. Even the towns and villages are built on terraces, and also the whole area is teaming with the Nazis, who will not give it up without a fight!"

Devastation of war, and lo, a *miracle*, in Europe 1943

Chapter 4
Victory, and Return to England

The day of August 19, 1943, brought a beautiful red twilight and sunrise over the rocky crags of the Italian mainland, as Smith and I left the mess tent and reported for duty. "Buzz," Tommy Smith spoke out, "I hope this ain't the day that we cross that Strait and climb onto that boot!" "Tommy," I answered, "I don't think that it's going to happen that way. I think that when Italy is invaded, a better beachhead will be selected by our commanders!"

As we walked into the medical supply tent, Lieutenant Gray called us over to his desk where a group of our medics were waiting patiently. "Men," he said, "since the outfit to which we were attached is slated for transfer and will not take part in future Mediterranean operations, we will be orphaned again as a Casual Company. However, tomorrow we will all travel by truck to Catania where we are badly needed aboard a hospital ship as hospital orderlies on her voyage to the United Kingdom.

On the day of August 20, 1943, this group of orphaned field medics arrived in Catania, which was on central Sicily's east coast, close-by the Ionian Sea. Catania had fallen to the British troops of Field Marshal Montgomery's Eighth Army, only days before. Upon arrival alongside the hospital ship's mooring, we all boarded within the hour along with our duffel bags and field equipment. After a hasty breakfast of Spam, powdered eggs, and dishwater coffee, we were assigned to our quarters. Tommy spoke up at this time, "Buzz, at least we got a bunk, such as it is, with canvas laced onto steel piping." "Right you are, Tommy," I answered, "and don't leave out the luxury of cork-filled life jackets we can use for pillows!" The ship loaded with mostly wounded allied troops, plus some heavily guarded Italian and German POWs, the vessel slipped out from her moorings just before midnight. The following morning, after breakfast, our medics were assigned the duties to take care of the needs of all patients on "C" deck. In other words, we assisted the nurses, filling in as hospital orderlies. On his first round of duty, Tommy took me aside saying, "Buzz, guess what? My first duty was 'bed pan commando' for four guys confined to their bunks!"

"Don't think you are the only one with that privilege. There were five on my rounds," was the answer I gave him as I went on about my duties.

At the end of this first day, after the sun had dipped below the western horizon of the Mediterranean and a full moon shown in the east, I paused against the rails of an outer deck to enjoy nature's beauty! All at once I felt that I wasn't alone, so I turned and standing close beside me was the cute little British nurse with whom I had been working, this first day of duty. "A penny for your thoughts, Yank, and may I join you in your lonely vigil," she blurted out, as the element of surprise engulfed me. To this I replied, "You do not have to buy my thoughts, little one, as they are not for sale at this time, too very stressful to talk about so soon after this costly conquest! The pleasure is all mine, if you care to join me in this admiration of the beauty of this tranquil sea, and this night sky full of stars, with a full moon to light our way, as danger lurks on every horizon." "Thank you, Yank, I respect your feelings, as I know what hell you have experienced, and I will join you in this appreciation of Mother Nature's creations that man can never duplicate!" She spoke softly, as we touched hands and stood silently against the rail, while the ship moved almost silently through this calm Mediterranean.

This British nurse, Mary, and I worked together on this entire voyage of twelve days. During off duty hours, we enjoyed each other's company, mostly on the open deck under moon and starlit skies, which brightened the mind as well as the universe in these trying times of World War II.

The day after this hospital ship passed through the Straits of Gibraltar, and made her northerly turn toward the Bay of Biscay, I bumped into my buddy, Tommy Smith. "Buzz," he said, "I haven't seen much of you lately. Where the hell have you been?" "Busy, Tommy, damn busy," I answered, "lots of work and long hours!" "Like hell, Buzz," he replied, "everybody knows you've been romancing that pretty little British nurse! You better watch that because she is an officer and you are a private, so you are treading on forbidden territory!" "Like hell I am," I shot back. "Mary likes my company, and I like hers, I can't get busted because I am already at the bottom, and they are surely not going to bust her, as nurses like her don't come around very often! Now bug off, Tommy, as I have a hell of a lot of work staring me in the face!"

I heard no more talk about my association with the little Lieutenant during the rest of this voyage, and the ship made arrival in Southampton, England, during the evening of September 1, 1943. We had no problems with the enemy for the entire voyage. With red crosses painted on the sides and decks of this large hospital ship, the enemy did show respect for the rules established at the Geneva Convention!

It was a sad day, September 2nd when I said farewell to Mary, who had been very special to me, and boarded a train with my group for probably another replacement depot! Not to our great surprise, the following day, September 3, 1943, our Casual Company arrived at the same damn replacement depot that we departed three months earlier, for assignment to wherever, we would be needed.

And yes, it was raining, the same Colonel kept us in pouring rain while he gave a monotonous speech, and after a cold chow, we retired to leaky tents!

Chapter 5
A New Assignment

I was designated to a food ration depot working in food ration breakdown and inventories. Within weeks I was writing menus for several army installations in the area, including a war office. In other words I was a Private doing a Lieutenant's work while he took it easy mostly, and stayed right in line to be awarded the Order of the Purple Bottom!

In February of 1944, I was really fit to be tied, when our Commanding Colonel approached me with a big smile on his ruddy face. "Soldier," he spoke out, "you have never had a furlough, so I am authorizing an eight-day one for you to London. Tomorrow a Lieutenant General will inspect your work area and if everything passes, you and your friend Sergeant Baroski will be on your way." "Fine, Colonel," I answered with a sharp salute, "my work area will pass, and all my inventories are up-to-date." With that he departed and I worked into the night making sure that all was in readiness for Lieutenant General Jacob L. Devers' inspection.

When the General arrived, I reported to him in a military manner, then escorted him around my entire food ration area where he checked for cleanliness along with all of my paper work and inventory sheets. Later the Colonel came by saying, "Soldier, you passed the General's inspection with flying colors. You and Sergeant Baroski have a good time in London."

Arriving in London the following day by train, Sergeant Baroski and I were greeted by the thickest pea soup fog imaginable, as the hundreds of barrage balloons were barely visible. We spent the first day exploring Piccadilly, Soho, and many other places of interest including Trafalgar Square, and a real comedy show at the famous Paladium Theatre.

When darkness descended upon this war-ravaged world capital, the air raid warnings sounded off; and the unmistakable drones of the Nazi bombers could be heard very clearly. In a short while the bombs began exploding close-by, amid a ceiling of bursting antiaircraft shells. Baroski and I entered a nearby air raid shelter which was a subway station, but seeing only two people inside, we went back on the street to the closest pub, and that is where all the people were.

After enjoying several Scotch and bitters, we met two pretty uniformed WAAFS (Women's Auxiliary Air Force) who were attached to the RAF (Royal Air Force) and we really had fun pub-crawling until the girls had to return to their billets at midnight. We could find no room at the big Red Cross Center of Rainbow Corners, so being Polish, Baroski was able to find us a room in the Knight's Bridge section of London at the Polish White Eagle Club. The room was shared with two Polish RAF pilots, and this was our hotel for the entire eight nights in London. Also, London's second blitz by the Nazi Luftwaffe began the first night of our arrival and continued every night.

The second day in London, Baroski and I departed the Polish Club for a sight-seeing tour of London. On our way, just across the street passing by the Hotel Alexandria, we could see that it was completely gutted by a direct bomb hit. Many beautiful buildings in the heart of London were the same way, just an empty shell.

On our tour, which was directed by the Red Cross, we toured Buckingham Palace, Number 10 Downing Street, Tower of London, London Bridge, the Houses of Parliament, Westminster Abbey, and St. Paul's Cathedral. Bombs had hit a wing of St. Paul's, but its beautiful dome was intact. What was so fantastic about St. Paul's is that it was standing alone like a sentinel amid blocks of total destruction! After this fantastic tour, Baroski and I attended a dance at Rainbow Corners which featured Glen Miller's Band and there were many beautiful girls there from all walks of life.

Every day left of this furlough was spent sight-seeing on our own through the streets of London, stopping off at restaurants and pubs, dining mostly on fish and chips, also downing many pints of room temperature strong English bitters. The Red Lion was one of our favorite pubs and meeting place with some of our new friends. Most of our nights were spent at the Polish Club Lounge enjoying food and Pivor (beer) with our Polish friends, both male and female, who were serving Poland in the RAF. This was also a safer place to be from flying shrapnel during the nightly air raids and dancing to the native Polish music made one forget imminent dangers.

When day eight came around, the Sergeant and I departed famous Paddington Station (which had really taken a beating from the blitz), arriving in Gloucestershire just as darkness fell on this city. It had been a wonderful furlough, which would be the last on my overseas duty of two years, plus. In this fair city on the River Severn of which Baroski and I were very familiar, we went to an ancient pub for a couple of pints before returning to camp, which was nearby. This pub was "The Monk's Retreat" at the end of a closed tunnel, which in centuries past was used by monks who followed the underground tunnel from the famous Gloucestershire Cathedral across the wide street to relax with their daily pint. While there in this ancient pub, I met a very pretty nurse from the Island of Malta who was having a "shanty" (lemonade and beer). This was where Baroski and I said good-night as he was very tired and decided to return to camp early.

Anita invited me to a party and dance at an open, dimly lit courtyard, attended by medical personnel from the hospital to which she was assigned. As the night came on, a beautiful full moon came into view on the eastern horizon. Anita (tired after a full day at her hospital) turned to me saying, "Senor, shall we walk down to the River Severn and enjoy the beauty of this moon and starlit night?" I then gave this Maltese senorita my answer, "yes, by all means!" It was beautiful down by the Severn, as we talked and got to know each other better in this fantastic atmosphere along the River's high grassy banks. Time passed very quickly, and after escorting Anita back to her billets, I just had enough time to catch the 0200 train back to the town close to my camp.

In my bunk by 0300, I was called at 0500 to begin my military duties of the day. After a quick breakfast, I encountered Baroski coming into the mess. "Have a nice time with the pretty Maltese nurse who captured you?" "Yes," I replied. "I think you two were meant to cross paths, from the way you looked at each other when you met. I thought the electricity would shock hell out of me when I walked between you two as I left last night." With that remark I shook my head, as I headed for the food storage area and my twelve hours of duty coming up. In the past I had been dating a pretty Welch lass, but she had gone home to Wales, so it could not have been a better time for Anita to come along.

When my workday was over, I wrote out passes for my group and had the Lieutenant sign them. Then I showered, donned my uniform, and met Annie on time at The Golden Fleece Inn, which was close-by her billet. I found out a lot about this Maltese beauty this memorable night. She had lived with her grandmother in a small stone house on a green hillside above Valetta, Malta, which was one of the world's most bombed cities and seaports during World War II. Annie wanted to be a nurse in order to help the war wounded, so was sent to the "Mother Country, England." Here she became a much needed British Army nurse in the field. Annie's time in England was coming to an end too soon, as in two weeks she would graduate as a field hospital nurse, to be assigned to the British Eighth Army in Italy.

We knew that this was an all out war of liberation, so I told her about plans that I had made to volunteer for combat training. "We both can see that continental Europe is going to experience one of the greatest invasions in world history," I told her. "We do not know at what hour this will take place, but I do want to be part of this history. I didn't come all this distance to continue rationing food and writing menus, so right away I am putting in for a transfer." To this she answered, "my wonderful soldier, I love you for the courage you show to really leave the secure duty you have and volunteer for the hell of battle in the front lines. Remember, if you are wounded and become disabled, I will always care for you, but we hope this never happens. I pray we will both survive this great war and live to meet again, we must always write and keep in touch!" "This will take place," I replied, "as we do have very strong feelings for each other!" I was actually falling in love with this remarkable young Maltese girl, and I knew from her actions that the feeling was mutual. This beautiful moonlit night, again by the murmuring Severn River, she declared her love for me. The night turned into early morning before I escorted Annie to her billet and returned to camp.

The following day I talked with the Colonel as he made a tour of inspection. He wanted me to continue my work here, but I was firm in my commitment to fight the war on the field of battle.

For the next two weeks Annie and I spent many wonderful hours together making plans to meet again at the war's end. Then there came the night when there was no Annie at our meeting place. As I turned to depart for her billet, a nice lady handed me a letter. The letter was from Annie, who had departed in early morning under secrecy to a port of embarkation for the voyage to Italy.

    The following two weeks after Annie's departure, I pulled almost every string in the book in order to get my transfer for combat infantry training and assignment. Finally, one day I was called to the Company Commander's office. When I arrived in the orderly room, the clerk spoke out with a big smile on his face, "looks like you may get your wish, the Captain will see you now, so knock and walk in!" I walked into the CO's office, came to attention, saluted, and spoke in a strong voice saying, "Captain, Private Rice reporting on orders!" "At ease, soldier, have a seat as I have good news for you! Your transfer will become effective in thirty days. During that time you will train another soldier to take over your duties in ration breakdown. I don't know why you are leaving this safe, secure position, but I know you have your reasons, and I really do commend you for this! I am a Captain of Infantry, as you know, so I also expect to be assigned in the future to combat duty! May we meet again and good luck!" "Thank you, Captain," I said, as I saluted and returned to my assigned duties. The following day a young soldier reported to me for training in my line of work. He was a good worker, and learned quickly, so in thirty days, "Vic" was well qualified to take up my duties.

    During the first week of May 1944, I was all packed on this bright sunny morning waiting for the jeep ride to the railroad station when mail call took place. This was my day, as I received mail from home, and also three letters from Annie. The Company driver picked me up about this time, so I didn't get to open my mail until about an hour later after being settled in my train compartment and on the way to Tidworth, England, close-by Salisbury. The letters from home told me that all was well there, and the long awaited letters from Annie were a big boost to my morale. She had arrived in Italy safely, after her ship had been torpedoed just before reaching Naples. She was very fortunate to be rescued, along with many others, by a American ship. Annie was set up in a field hospital, so she had been, and still was close enough to the front lines to receive enemy fire!

Arriving in Tidworth at 2200 hours, it was still daylight when a jeep driver picked me up at the train station and delivered me to a tent area out in the middle of nowhere! More trainees were arriving from other areas of England, so everyone was assigned to their designated tent with a folding cot and mattress cover filled with straw. After everything settled down, a meal of Spam, dehydrated mashed potatoes, and peas with "seconds" available, was served just as darkness shrouded this bleak tent city. When the late meal was over, close to midnight, a Lieutenant came into the mess tent and filled us in on the information which all of us needed. "Men, listen up," he spoke in a loud voice, "most of you have volunteered but some have been sent here from replacement depots. You will all receive rugged training in combat infantry tactics which will begin in two weeks. In the meantime, you will be issued combat gear including an M-1 rifle, duties will be KP, and guard duty in which you will be issued live ammunition. You will also at all times be prepared for quarters, personal and rifle inspections. Passes will be issued each day from 1700 to 2400 for places close-by, which includes Tidworth, Amesbury or Salisbury, but once your training begins, that situation will come to a halt! Now, at ease, and have a good night's sleep, because you must be tired as hell, tomorrow and reveille will come too damn quick, 0500 in case you are interested!"

From the first day, after reveille and breakfast chow, I was assigned to food preparation in the large field kitchen as a "KP" pusher. This assignment continued for a week, with duty lasting twelve hours a day, and a six-hour pass every night to go into Amesbury enjoying the sights with some new acquaintances. As the week ended on Saturday, I had a twenty-four hour pass for Salisbury. After about an hour's ride on an old steam-powered English bus, I arrived in this beautiful old city, with the world famous cathedral. What a fantastic sight Salisbury Cathedral was, with its gigantic spires reaching high into the fog-shrouded skies. At noon the fog lifted, the sun came out just as I departed The Robinhood Pub and headed for a "fish and chip" shop. While enjoying fish and chips at the counter, a pretty RAF WAAF started up a conversation. When lunch was over, we left the shop together, as it turned out we were both going to visit Stonehenge which is located a fair distance away on the Salisbury Plain. She and I joined a group of service personnel and civilians for a tour of this fantastic, as well as a very mysterious place, in another of the wartime charcoal- and steam-powered busses. "Yank," she asked, " 'ave you never seen before our pre-historical Stonehenge?" "No," I answered, "but I hear it is very intriguing. A mystery to this day that has never been solved. I believe that in centuries beyond recall, when Druids roamed the British Isles they left behind a remembrance of their once intelligent existence." Then 'ow did they arrange the stones as such?" she asked with a smile. To this question as we were now within sight of this unusual place, I answered, "the legendary Druids were a very smart and mysterious people, like the ancient Egyptians, they probably used the ancient art of leverage!" "You, my Yankee friend, are a legend in your time," she said, "and your belief in fantasy actually intrigues me to no end!" As we all departed the old steam bus and walked in the quiet mystery surrounding these legendary arrangements of gigantic stones, one could imagine the time-consuming labor required to construct whatever this was.

With the passing of an hour, we all boarded the ageless bus, arriving back in Salisbury just in time to welcome the two-hour evening opening of the pubs. The WAAF Betty and I had a couple of pints each of the warm bitters before the pub owner of the Robinhood called time on beer and started pushing "Old Scrump" (cider) which was strong enough to walk down the street by itself! At 2200 hours (ten o'clock) the pub keeper yelled out "Time, ladies and gentlemen, please drink up and turn in your glosses." Betty and I then had fish and chips in the closest shop, and afterwards, a walk through a beautiful park. We were late arriving back at the bus stop, but she managed to get a taxi back to her billets. After saying our farewells, I hurried to where the last bus would leave Salisbury for my camp, but I managed only to see it's taillights disappear around a curve way ahead. I really didn't know just what the hell to do when all at once an army truck stopped and the driver asked directions to Tidworth. "I'm heading that way and will be glad to show you directions," I answered happily! "Then hop in and let's get going, soldier, be glad to have your company!" It turned out that the truck had supplies for my training camp, so within my pass time frame, I was home free and in the sack by 0100 hours.

Reveille came too damn soon at 0500 hours this Monday morning, but I was ready to take on the day. After breakfast chow, my Company had continuous drills along with a manual of arms and rifle inspection until noon. Following lunch chow, my platoon was allowed to rest during the afternoon, as all of us would be assigned to roving guard duty with live ammunition from 1800 to 0600, a full twelve hours. This same routine continued each day and night for the entire week, with only about six hours rest in twenty-four. We were being toughened up for the combat training just days ahead. Also, the roving guard security was totally necessary, as an infantry division along with other combat troops were moving out of the area continually night and day!

Something big was about to happen, as all of these troop movements toward English ports made the threat of invasion on continental Europe a reality. How I wished that our Company could be part of this history, but after future training, we would join the drive to free this enslaved continent from the bonds of Naziism.

With Sunday, came a day of rest which was much appreciated and was treated as such, because the following weeks would bring a very rough schedule of advanced combat training. After sleeping all day, the Company was called for dinner chow, which turned out to be steak, french fries, and peas, a real gourmet feast from what we had been accustomed. Our diet in the past weeks had consisted mostly of C rations, lamb, goat, beans, and brussel sprouts. When this meal was finished the Mess Sergeant called, "seconds!" I then got the hell out of the mess hall, as one could be trampled in the rush of these "chow hounds." My buddy, Hoffman, joined me in this fast retreat, speaking out, "fattening up for the kill! Let's get the hell out of here, buddy, hop over the fence and spend this last night in the village, pub-crawling with the locals. We can pull this off, hop back over the fence and make 'bed check' by 2300. After all, with no moon, it will be dark enough to cast no telltale shadows." "OK, Hoff," I answered, "agreed, it's our last night's fling and we can do it!" This caper worked out exactly as planned, we had no big problems getting out, enjoyed several pints of bitters with the locals and made 'bed check'." A guard stopped us coming back, but didn't report the incident, as there were quite a few more of the same occurring this night of restriction before the war games began!

Chapter 6
Let the War Games Begin

This Monday morning, the first day of my combat training, began with a call out (reveille) at 0400 hours. This day was welcomed in with a thick cloud cover and a cold driving rain. After a forced march of five miles, our Company reached the location of a field kitchen on the rain-drenched Salisbury Plain. As we marched up to this much appreciated site, a mean-looking Mess Sergeant yelled out "OK youse guys, break out your damn mess kits and form a double line. This is the only damn hot meal you gonna get for the next damn week, so enjoy this gourmet breakfast!" The "gourmet breakfast" turned out to be scrambled powdered eggs, fried Spam, oatmeal, and British brown bread. The strong coffee was best of all, as it, along with this "gourmet" food warmed to the soul of these tired, cold and wet infantry trainees at 0600 in the morning on this dreary Salisbury Plain.

When the meal was over, our tough Second Lieutenant Garcia yelled out, "OK men, off your asses and on your feet! After washing your mess kits, line up in a column of two's, shoulder your packs and rifles and let's get the hell going, as we got thirty more miles to go before we bivouac for the night!" From 0700 to 1200 we marched through the pouring rain, then on orders from the Company Commander, our unit broke for lunch, which turned out to be "K" rations. This consisted of a small can of cheese, chocolate-oatmeal bar, hard crackers, lemon powder (for lemonade), two cigarettes, and toilet paper. When this lunch was consumed by 1230, orders were the same "off and on!" Marching through this soggy wet countryside until 1900 hours, our Company finally reached the bivouac area, as bleak a place that could be imagined, even on the Salisbury Plain! Called to attention after a brief break, the Lieutenant had us doing the Manual of Arms for an hour, until everyone was in perfect unison. When the order came to "fall out," I know that damn nearly everyone felt just like the two words meant. Our Platoon Sergeants then paired us off, and as each man carried a tent pole and shelter half in his field pack, pup tents for two were set up for the night. Each man was then issued a box of "K" rations which this time consisted of a small can of corned pork, dried fruit bar, four hard crackers, Nescafe, two cigarettes, and toilet paper. After chow, everybody was so damn exhausted that the pup tents on the soggy ground even looked inviting as we crawled in, clothes, boots and all, then literally passed out.

Awakened by the reveille bugler at 0500 hours the following morning, the Company was called to attention, then each Platoon was lined up in a column of two's and did "double time" for two miles before breakfast chow. This "K" ration consisted of a small can of ham and eggs, four hard crackers, chocolate-oatmeal bar, and Nescafe, also the two cigarettes and toilet paper were included. When this breakfast chow was over, it was "off your asses and on your feet" again, and our whole Company (after packing our equipment) was forced marched until reaching an obstacle course at noon, with only two five-minute breaks in six hours. A half-hour break was allowed for our lunch "K" ration (which was the same as yesterday), then each Platoon was lined up and with full field pack and rifle, went through the entire obstacle course. This was a mean course and it consisted of every type of obstacle that a human being could imagine, to wear the hell out of a combatant. We climbed cargo nets, swung over streams on ropes, crawled through culverts, and mastered many other obstacles, then we "about faced" and did the whole damn thing again! Tired as hell after regrouping again, our unit was marched another five miles, where we set up our pup tents again, and this time "C" rations were handed out, these consisted of a can of meat and vegetable stew, hard crackers, a can of fruit, chocolate, and the traditional sample pack of cigarettes along with daily paper. Our latrines were slit trenches which were dug on arrival and covered upon departure from the area. The compact "pick-mattock" shovels (which were carried at all times in the field) were used for the purpose of digging everything from slit trenches to foxholes.

The next morning, after a fitful night of sleep in water two inches deep, due to a pouring rain, reveille was held at 0500 hours. With clothes sticking to our bodies, another "K" ration breakfast was consumed before lining up in a column of two's and marching out. After another twenty-five mile forced march, with two five-minute breaks in between, our Company arrived at an "infiltration course." With thirty minutes break for a "K" ration lunch, we spent the rest of the day crawling on our bellies and attacking an unseen enemy. During this whole episode, live ammunition along with exploding shells were too close for comfort. Finishing up at the "infiltration course," we covered another five miles before our bivouac area was reached. Once our pup tents were set up, "C" rations were handed out, and a bunch of dog-tired GIs really savored this meager chow as if it were a festive event! When this "gourmet" dinner was finished, the whole damn Company was so exhausted that all we could do was crawl into our pup tents and pass out! Along about midnight our tough First Sergeant Luciano's voice rang out over the megaphone, "OK youse guys, off your asses and on your feet, break down your pup tents and fall out in ten minutes with full field pack!" To this order we complied, and after closing the slit trenches, the whole damn area was policed before the Company was called to attention and marched out in a column of two's with shouldered arms.

During our first five-minute break, my buddy Hoffman said to me, "Buzz (my nickname), this is one hell of a way to live, but you know we are bound to it until we are wounded, killed in action, or be lucky enough to finish the duration of this damn war." "Damn well right you are, Hoff," I answered, "I really do hope and pray that we will be fortunate enough to see that fantastic day when all of Europe will be liberated from the damn Nazis." Hoffman's reply was, "Buzz, you know I am Jewish and was born in Germany, lived there until the Nazis gained power, then escaped before the Holocaust swallowed me up. I will never surrender to the Nazi pigs, because to them I would still be a Jewish citizen and placed before a firing squad or sent to the gas chambers." To this I stated, "Hoffman, I hope we are sent to the same outfit when we finish this combat training. Even though I am a protestant, I consider you a brother and feel the same as you; together, we will be a hell of a combat team, and the Nazis will damn well know that the two of us have been around!" "Thanks, Buzz," Hoffman answered, "we are brothers and will continue to be so in this coming up liberation of continental Europe from the damn Nazi noose."

The order rang out from our First Sergeant at this time, which was the same as always, "off your asses and on your feet, shoulder arms and march out in a column of two's!" Another three hours of marching through the dank, wind- and rain-swept moors, all Platoons were called to a halt. "OK men, fall out for chow. Gourmet 'K' rations will again be the menu for breakfast, so enjoy!"

After thirty minutes, all Platoons of the Company were called to attention, then marched out to an area two miles distant where a group of tanks and half-tracks were located at strategic points. The rest of this day, each Platoon was broken up and we mounted at times the half-tracks, rode on them, then mounted and rode the Sherman tanks, training in armored infantry tactics. We trained with bazooka experts and learned to load and fire this rocket launcher from the shoulder, to knock out enemy positions. Also, we were trained to use this weapon in disabling and knocking out the Nazis Tiger tanks by hitting them at their weakest points. This training continued all day until 2000 hours, when our company was regrouped, called to attention, and marched out in a column of two's to the fabulous sight of a field kitchen. This was unbelievable, as once we reached the end of the serving line, our mess kits were loaded with swiss steak, mashed potatoes, red beans, and brussel sprouts, also our canteen cups contained hot java. After about fifteen minutes, the Mess Sergeant yelled, "seconds!" This magic word really created a mad rush and anyone in these chow hounds' path stood a damn good chance of being trampled! There is nothing that will warm up to the soul of a nearly exhausted infantry Company than good hot chow with strong hot java to wash it down. With this real gourmet chow over, our Company was marched another two miles to a bivouac area where pup tents were pitched and all hit the sack!

The next day, to our great surprise, our Company was greeted at early reveille by a fantastic dawn, as the sun cleared the eastern horizon spreading its healing rays over this barren moor. The day began with the traditional breakfast of "K" ration, break up of the bivouac area, and marching off with all equipment. This group of trainees were being pushed to the hilt, in order to get us well trained for battle. Something big was about to take place and it was written on the faces of every officer and soldier! Again, our Company trained all day in armored infantry tactics, riding the rumbling tanks and hopping off to clear the way of unseen enemy strongholds, as we advanced ever forward.

During the next several days our Company continued these armored infantry tactics with half-tracks and tanks. In the near future we would be sent as replacements to armored divisions that would be spearheading for advancing allied armies, so it was a dire necessity that we be trained to perfection! The M-1 rifle was our standby, but we were also trained in the days ahead to use heavy firepower. This consisted of the use of Thompson sub-machine guns, the thirty- and fifty-caliber machine guns, Browning automatic rifles, then, of course, the always handy grenades, along with bazookas.

As we participated in these advanced training exercises, "Operation Overlord" took place on June 6, 1944. The greatest invasion in history began at 0100 hours as paratroopers landed in Normandy, followed later by the gigantic amphibious invasion of Allied ground forces! The long awaited liberation of the Nazi enslaved countries of continental Europe had finally begun, and from all reports, the Allies had a good foothold by nightfall.

As these brave men advanced in Normandy, our Company was still in advanced armored infantry training tactics in the English countryside. With the training we were undergoing both day and night, each of us would be well-prepared to perform in any combat outfit of future assignment. Our training continued for two more weeks and became more and more complex as we moved with the tanks both day and night, using all types of weapons. We were being prepared for the real thing, and it was accepted as such, because our lives depended on this knowledge of warfare. Days and nights into the early morning hours, we practiced patrols ahead of the tanks, both recon and combat patrols, and each of us took our place at the head of the patrol as "point man," (the one who draws enemy fire first).

Finally during the last week in June, our battlefield training would let up. After two days on the firing range, Hoffman and I both made "expert" firing the M-1 rifle, thirty- and fifty-caliber machine guns, the B.A.R. (Browning automatic rifle), carbine, Thompson sub-machine gun and bazooka. We, along with a score of other GIs in the company, were awarded the Expert Infantry Badge.

As the first week in July came around, commando and paratrooper training took place at a British facility with the "Tommies." This last training phase was guaranteed to separate the men from the boys, but everyone came through and mastered this tough course in an excellent manner. The British food wasn't the best at this place, but it was hot and healthy, with the traditional tea at every meal. Breakfast consisted of windbreakers (beans) on toast, and after a rough training day, the goat or lamb stew, brown bread, and hot tea were very much welcomed by these very tired soldiers!

Once all of this advanced infantry training came to an end during the middle of July, our Company was transported to a tent city staging area north of Southhampton. Once there, we cleaned up, shaved, and discarded our old clothes. New (OD) uniforms were issued along with combat jackets, combat boots, cartridge belts, and bayonets. New M-1 rifles were issued, but were loaded with a thick coat of Cosmoline, which required hours to clean off, piece by piece with gasoline. Now, with all of our training accomplished, and new uniforms, along with combat equipment issued, our Company was officially on standby as replacements in combat. There were all sorts of rumors floating around that we may be flown in as replacements in the airborne infantry, or seaborne to Normandy where the newly formed Third Army was making history! Anyway, the whole outfit was restricted, so until orders came in to move out, we would be pulling KP and guard duty strictly in this tent city.

On a Friday morning in the third week of July 1944, just as we came off guard duty, the tough Lieutenant told Hoffman and myself that we would be given a twenty-four hour pass to London. "The last damn one youse guys are going to get," he said, "cause the two of youse are shipping out next week!" There was no need to ask any questions, because we wouldn't be told a damn thing anyway, due to strict secrecy!

Hoffman and I really jumped at this chance to enjoy the wonders of London, so when the passes were issued, along with several other guys, we caught a Jeep ride to the station, and were shortly aboard the London express. Upon arrival in London, it was late morning, so we knew the pubs would be open until 1400 hours, and no time was lost getting to the Red Lion. After drinking several pints of bitters with two A.T.S. (Army Territorial Service) girls, who were very friendly, the pub keeper called out: "time, ladies and gentlemen, please," so the four of us departed to enjoy this great city's sights. This was a pretty day, so we spent the rest of it taking in the scenic areas along the Thames. There were some nice pubs and sidewalk cafes along the park like Thames estuary and I think we visited everyone of them. When "time, please" was called out at the Blue Peter pub, close-by the East India docks at 2200 hours (10:00 p.m.) we went to a park area, where one could watch a beautiful sunset at this time of year just before midnight. There were dangerous fireworks to watch also, as antiaircraft flak was exploding over parts of the city due to pilotless V-1 rockets (buzz bombs) dropping at random, in order to bring more Nazi terror and destruction to the British.

During the short night, by a full moon, we all stayed in the park area by the River Thames, as ships and barges passed in review. Also several of the "buzz bombs" that made it through the maze of flak over the city, caused huge explosions where they landed. A few were hit by flak, and when this happened it seemed that the universe had exploded! As the morning sun showed its brilliant upper limb over the horizon above the Thames, it was a picture that only Mother Nature could produce. Across the River, in London proper, the night fog was lifting like a curtain, revealing the Houses of Parliament, Big Ben, and St. Paul's Cathedral still along among blocks of total destruction. The maze of barrage balloons was ever prevalent!

The very next double-decker bus that came along the four of us flagged it down, crossed London Bridge, and rode all the way to Piccadilly. Stopping off at Rainbow Corners Red Cross Club, all of used the facilities there to wash up, shave, and get ready for the day ahead. After a breakfast of coffee, tea, and fresh doughnuts, we were ready for this beautiful day. It turned out to be a great day, except for the random touchdown and explosion of several of the Nazi rocket specialists calling cards, the dreaded V-1 buzz bombs. This day was really filled with excitement as the four of us explored the timeless streets of the seedy sections of old London. Long lines (queues) of housewives were prevalent at shops in the market areas, for food of all kinds, mainly fish. Hoffman asked one of the ladies at the end of one queue, "Lady, is this the queue for bile beans?" The lady turned around with a disgusted look and blurted out, " 'ell no, Yank, it's for 'aving a baby test, would you be joining us?" That answer really took the wind out of Hoffman, and all had a spell of laughter as we continued on down this ancient street called "Petticoat Lane."

Finally, a little after noon, our group reached the Red Lion pub in the heart of the city, where we dined on vegetable sandwiches washed down with strong Guiness Stout. When "time, please" was called out at the Red Lion, it was 1400 hours (2:00 p.m.) and time for Hoffman and me to depart for camp. The A.T.S. lassies went with us to Paddington Station where we were seen off on our destiny with a very positive farewell kiss, and a "V" for victory sign. As the train steamed off, traveling at a high rate of speed through the English countryside, stopping at several townships during the late afternoon, Hoff and I finally reached our destination. We stopped at a pub called the King's Head to have a couple pints of bitters, staying until "time, please" was called. Walking to camp, which was about three miles from town we finished devouring two large orders of fish and chips, wrapped in English newspapers. It was still twilight when we arrived at the main gate before our passes would expire at midnight, and within a few minutes we were in our sacks snoring away!

Reveille sounded at 0500 in the morning which was Sunday, and might have been a day of rest, except for special plans the Commander had for us! With the company at "parade rest," our Company Commander made the following announcement: "First Platoon, Attention! You have been selected by the Camp Commander to perform at a parade today in a very aristocratic English township. The parade you will be a part of is an Army contingent that will pass in review before many military and civilian dignitaries. Now at ease! All Platoons fall out, breakfast chow will be served in the mess tent!" Hoffman looked at me and spoke out, "Buzz, why in hell's name has our Platoon been singled out for this?" My answer to this was, "Hoffman, the reason is very obvious, because we are the best, so let's wash up and chow down, as it's going to be one hell of a day!"

It was 0600 on this Sunday morning, after a hasty chow, that the First Platoon fell out in full dress ODs with rifles. Called to attention by our tough Lieutenant Garcia, we marched out in a single column to a line of GI trucks. Once aboard the trucks, we traveled over miles of country roads to this ancient and beautiful city, which had the most fantastic wide, treelined promenade any of us had ever seen, Cheltenham, in the ancient Cotswold.

Dismounting the big trucks, our Platoon joined many other combat units at the head of this promenade. In front of all units was the United States Army band with colors waving in the light breeze. Called to: "Attention! Right shoulder arms!" We were led by the Army band, this vast parade of combat infantry passed in review before a group of very important dignitaries observing from a roof garden, halfway down this fabulous promenade. There were two American Generals, a British Air Marshal, the King and Queen of England, Princess Elizabeth (who then was an A.T.S. Colonel), Queen Wilhelmina, King Haakon of Norway, and several more VIPs watching our performance. When this great parade was over, the dignitaries gave us an outstanding mark of perfection!

After this day's activities were over, all were given an hour break for refreshments, then my Platoon was called to "attention" and marched at "right shoulder arms" to a side street and the trucks, which we mounted for the ride back. This had been a very busy, also hectic day for our Platoon, so when we arrived back at tent city, and found out that it was completely restricted, all were fit to be tied! After dinner chow, which was served in the mess tent, Lieutenant Garcia broke down and issued those of us in the First Platoon, four-hour passes for the local village which would be patrolled by Military Police. When this good news circulated around, Hoffman yelled out, "After all we got damn good guy, this Lieutenant Garcia, he's tops in my book, anybody that don't go to the pubs tonight is horse's patootie!" "OK, Hoff," I answered, "you've had your say, so let's get the hell out of here, so we can down a few pints before the barmaid at the Black Dog Inn calls "time, please."

While sitting at a back room table in the crowded inn with two old Cockney-speaking codgers, downing pints of warm English bitters brought by the barmaid, Hoff and I listened to one of them tell about an experience he had recently. "Matey's," he said, "Oi drives me 'orse and wagon in me workdays, bringing 'oggseads of bitters and Old Scrump (cider) to pubs around the county. One day last week 'oi dropped off a 'oggsead of bitters at the 'Aire and 'Ounds pub in the village, 'od a spot of bitters meself, then 'ops on me wagon. 'Coo blimey, 'oi couldn't get the damn beast to move a'tall. 'Ofter trying everyway 'oi knew to get me 'oss to move, 'oi goes up the footpoth to the village 'oss doctor. Well, 'e gives me a red pill first, if 'e don't move, give 'im the green one!" The old codger's buddy very excitedly asked, "Did you 'im the red pill first like the 'oss doctor said, did 'e move ofter?" The old codger's answer was, "Did 'e move! Me 'oss moved so damn fast ofter 'oi give 'im the red pill, that if 'oi 'adn't taiken the green one meself 'id never of caught 'im!" That brought a good laugh to everyone, so I asked them to drink up and had the pretty barmaid set up another round at our table. These Britons were a very witty people and friendly beyond words. This was our platoon's last night out, so all of us loaded up on bitters, then Old Scrump, when "time" was called on bitters. All pubs and streets were cleared of GIs by the MPs when 2300 hours came about. We were all feeling so good that Hoffman's and my group walked all the way back to tent city singing "Danny Boy" so damn loud that it may have been heard across the Channel, where we would be heading on the morrow!

The following day, Monday, at 0500 reveille, the Company was given the following orders by our Company Commander. "Men, you will pack all of your gear and fall out at 0700 hours with full field packs, along with shouldered arms (rifles). You will then board trucks which will take you to the port of embarkation. Now fall out for breakfast chow in the mess tent. Mail call will follow chow!" Hoffman spoke up on the way to chow, "Buzz, I hope to hell we have decent breakfast, as one hell of a day is coming up for us!" "Don't worry, Hoff," I answered, "it's going to be a good one this time, because you know they always fatten you up for the kill!" "How nice of you, Buzz, to be so positive, that remark really makes my day," replied Hoffman. I was correct about this chow, as it consisted of fried steak, powdered eggs, hot cakes with syrup, and coffee strong enough to walk. Mail call followed chow, and I received letters from home and four letters from "Annie." All was well at home with my parents and my brothers, one in the Fifth Army, and the other in the South Pacific with the Marines, were holding their own. "Annie" was having it rough in the field hospital, close up front, in the rough Italian terrain, with the British Eighth Army.

Falling out with full field pack and equipment at the specified time, our whole well trained Combat Infantry Company was loaded on trucks and moved out on a mission to join combat units already on the fields of battle to free an enslaved continent!

I was really looking forward to putting this special training to good use on the battlefields of Europe. My friend, Hoffman, was just as anxious as I was to get in on this crusade to liberate France first, then onward to victory over the infamous Third Reich. Not to be underestimated was the tough Lieutenant Garcia, who also was on the verge of hysteria to get into the drive that would stem the flow of Naziism throughout Europe and the world. Lieutenant Garcia was a fast friend of all in our Platoon, as well as our leader, and was highly respected. He would not ask anyone to do something that he would not do himself, and that alone proved his immaculate leadership! Lieutenant Garcia was going to do his best to keep himself, Hoffman and me together when we went into combat as replacements. Hoffman and I were in line to be promoted to squad leaders when the occasion would come up!

The tide was turning rapidly in favor of Allied Armies in France, as troops of the United States First Army were advancing in face of fanatical Nazi resistance. Our planes also were playing havoc with the V-1 and V-2 rocket sites, destroying many. On July 17th Field Marshal Irwin Rommel's staff car was strafed by Allied planes, badly wounding and putting this famous Wehrmacht and Panzer leader out of commission. Then, after the breakthrough at St. Lo, General Patton's newly grouped Third Army was making history in the advance across Normandy toward the Avranches corridor. Total victory would be forthcoming, so let it be written!

Chapter 7
Arrival in France and Drive Into History

Upon arrival at a staging area close-by Southhampton, England, the whole company was broken up. The lot of us were now "'cannon fodder" replacements and would be shipped out to combat units in France where we were badly needed! After a meal of Spam, dehydrated mashed potatoes, and peas, we all were tired as hell, so we filled our mattress covers with available straw, then hit the sack.

The following morning at 0400 hours, reveille took place, then everyone lined up for breakfast chow. Within an hour Lieutenant Garcia, Hoffman, and I finally got our mess kits filled with powdered eggs, salted ham, mush and brown bread, and java like thirty-weight motor oil, but hot. The three of us had our breakfast together, then upon reaching our tent area, all replacements were ordered to "fall out" for routine inspection and further orders. After the inspection by an Army Captain, who seemed pleased by the results, we were allowed to "fall out" to the tents after the order "parade rest" was given. At 0800 hours, all the replacements in our area were ordered to "fall out" with full field packs, duffel bag, and rifles "on the double!" None of us wasted any time in doing so, and after being called to "attention" along with "right shoulder arms," we were once more marched out, loaded on trucks, and moved out. This time our destination was the port area where we dismounted and were marched to an LST (Landing Ship Tank) which was already taking on tanks as well as troops by the busloads! Lieutenant Garcia, Hoffman, and I found a spot by the ship's afterhouse to stash our gear and make ourselves as comfortable as possible on the steel deck. When the ship made departure from the dock, heading into the River Test, it was exactly 1700 hours (5:00 p.m.). As no hot food would be forthcoming, we dined for the second time this day on the old standby, "K" rations. It was 2300 hours (11:00 p.m.) when this ship reached the English Channel, after passing by Portsmouth and the Isle of Wight, the sun had just disappeared over the western horizon. Darkness came very quickly as this vessel plunged into the rough waters of this vast Channel with a full capacity of tanks and troops! Showing no lights, this vessel was shrouded in flying salt spray, as the deep-throated diesel engines kept her at full ahead, on this dangerous zig-zag crossing.

Everyone slept fitfully during the short period of darkness and when I awoke at 0330 hours, dawn was beginning to break in the eastern sky, bringing into view ships of all types, plying the same course as this LST. At our breakfast of "K" rations with Nescafe made from hot water furnished by a galley cook who befriended us, we learned that a Nazi torpedo had barely missed us, and also several magnetic mines were sighted. The LST continued on its course in these choppy waters, and during the midmorning hours, land was sighted, so Lieutenant Garcia alerted this group of replacements to get set for debarkation soon to take place.

The big LST hit the beach head-on at noon, close-by Sainte Mere-Eglise, Normandy, then her bow opened up and with ramp down, Sherman tanks began roaring out onto the cluttered landing area. All troops followed the route of the tanks, and were marched in a staggered single file to a bivouac area, where we set up pup tents and camouflaged them as best we could. Hoffman made the remark, "Well, Buzz, it won't be long now!" To this remark I answered, "Hoff, that's what the monkey said when his tail got caught in the lawn mower. Our next move will be to the front and we will be lucky if we keep ours intact." Lieutenant Garcia, Hoffman and all the other guys around who heard this remark had a damn good laugh, except for me, I was very serious.

We sacked out in our pup tents until 1700 hours (5:00 p.m.), when called out for evening chow. There were so many in the staggered chow line that Lieutenant Garcia, Hoffman and I didn't get our mess kits filled until 1900 (7:00 p.m.). Two damn hours of standing to get some damn chicken that looked like it had been boiled in bleach, beans half-cooked, and sick-looking beets along with overcooked spinach. The coffee was like dishwater, and so we all enjoyed our first meal in this war-ravaged French countryside. After finishing up our delicious meal, we sat around our designated areas, smoked from our free pack of Camels and shot the bull until darkness was upon us, then we hit the sack.

At first light the following morning a dozen replacements were called out. Hoffman and I were among these heading for the front, also Lieutenant Garcia. We were all issued live ammunition, (so with all our equipment) were loaded on half-tracks and tanks bound for the front. To me, this was like making history. France was being quickly liberated, and the great leader with the flair of Rommel, none other than General George S. Patton was already at the gates of Avranches. Patton's newly organized Third Army was sweeping around "der Fuehrer's" armies in Normandy, cutting off their supply lines, and those in our group were really excited to be a part of this history making advance.

Avranches fell from the Nazi grasp into the liberating hands of the United States Third Army on the day of our arrival, July 30, 1944. Our group replaced casualties in an armored spearhead of this victorious army and we rejoiced with the liberated French people who swarmed out to greet us as hostilities ended. Many of the German Wehrmacht surrendered here and were sent to the rear. Hoffman and I were assigned to an armored infantry company, and our new Platoon leader turned out to be none other than Lieutenant Garcia. Some of us rode on the outside of tanks, while others rode half-tracks as we moved through this city's narrow streets. Stopping at times, these newly liberated French showered us with confections they had saved for this occasion, including beaucoup vins and cognac, and beautiful mademoiselles greeted us with hugs and kisses!

The victorious United States troops were not allowed to tarry very long in Avranches, as time was critical in the armored drive to cut the enemy supply lines. Mopping up operations of enemy pockets, isolated by the fast moving armored spearhead, was taken over by regular infantry troops. Outside of the city our spearhead ran into some heavy resistance from the German Wehrmacht, Panzer (tank) units and the continuous bombardment of eighty-eight mm shells. One guy from Kentucky made the statement, "them Krauts can put an eighty-eight right in your hip pocket, and if you don't believe it, just stick your pocketbook back there!" Actually, he was damn nearly right, as they were a real scourge both day and night. The drive toward victory continued on, and soon the whole Brittany Peninsula was sealed off completely, leaving a full United States Division behind to keep it that way.

The hedgerows in western France were of utmost danger, as the enemy used them to their advantage in setting up ambushes. Every damn hedgerow in France was a deadly trap, as machine guns, mortars, snipers, and Tiger tanks lurked in their natural camouflage. The battle of the hedgerows took a heavy toll of American lives. In one instance, several of us were pinned down near a hedgerow, but one young GI from Virginia was in a spot where a movement would bring eternity, so in a high-pitched voice he spoke out, "one of you all please get that damn Kraut, if you don't get him, he's going to get me!" At that time several grenades were tossed in the machine gunner's direction, then the chatter of the gun ceased and all was quiet!

Regardless of every obstacle that came about, the armored spearheads continued to advance, and a sweep around the enemy armies in Normandy was taking place very fast, as the Third Army moved toward the great city of Orleans on the River Loire. In every town and village we passed through and liberated, the overly friendly French people gave us a jubilant welcome with hugs, kisses and beaucoup vins, cognac and calvados. At the same time, the townsfolk got together and shaved the heads of all girls who had fraternized with the Germans (Bosch).

War is really hell, but quite a few humorous things take place at times, also. As our outfit entered the Loire city of Orleans, the tank column Lieutenant Garcia, Hoffman, and I were assigned to was pinned down by heavy enemy fire from a seventy-ton King Tiger Panzer. Our squad was designated to knock out this enemy tank, so after cautiously getting behind this monster, we knocked out his engine and one track with two powerful bazooka rockets. The Nazis came out of the turret then, one by one, with hands over their helmets yelling, "comrade!" Then all of a sudden French citizens came rushing up yelling, "Bosch, no bon," and tried their best to take over our prisoners and gosh knows what. Anyway, we got the townspeople settled down and the prisoners were escorted back to join the thousands of their comrades. Before we moved on, some beautiful young girls came out, giving us all hugs and kisses! What a warm welcome! One beauty was kissing me as I was getting ready to mount the tank up front, and an old lady who was the girl's grandmother began beating me over the head with a hard loaf of French bread. I gave the young girl a pack of gum, and the grandmother a pack of cigarettes. After that the mademoiselle still continued kissing and the old lady stopped the loaf bit, smiled and said "American bon!"

After Orleans, General Patton swung his Third Army spearheads east toward the River Seine, in order to close the noose around the German armies. This was one hell of a drive, taking towns and villages along the way, arriving at the Seine, south of Paris on August 23, 1944. Two days later Paris fell to an American infantry division and a French armored division, along with the Free French Underground fighters who were not to be underestimated!

To the north of the Third Army position, news reached us that Field Marshal Montgomery's two armies had advanced over two hundred miles in four days. They were now sweeping through Belgium, as well as General Hodges' First Army, just to our north. The Nazis in France were in full retreat, so our Third Army under General Patton advanced very quickly to capture Reims, Verdun, Troyes, Chalons and bringing about many German casualties and capturing prisoners by the thousands. After Verdun, the armored spearhead continued onward, and the world's most fortified city, Metz, was pocketed off, and we finally reached the Moselle. Advancing down the western side of the Moselle from surrounded Metz, our Special Battalion and the Tank Battalion to which we were attached performed a strategic operation. We made a one hundred mile drive and helped bring the southern flank of the Third Army to the Belfort Gap. There at this strategic point, the Third and Seventh Armies were linked. At the Belfort Gap was my second encounter with one of my favorite Army Officers, Lieutenant General Jacob L. Devers, a Corps Commander. With the Belfort Gap operation in secure position, my special unit proceeded north to the area of Nancy, France, under orders from our Commander.

Both Hoffman and I had now been promoted to Line Sergeants, and were squad leaders in our Platoon, thanks to Lieutenant Garcia.

This advance was quickly initiated but it wasn't easy, as the Third Army ran into many pockets of resistance. Also, many casualties were suffered from the powerful German tanks which dwarfed our Shermans; however, we outmaneuvered them most of the time. The German 88 mm shells were also a hell of a weapon with which to combat, as were rocket shells called "screaming meemies" which tumbled through the sky causing a terrific scream before they hit and exploded. When we first experienced these harassing weapons, my buddy Hoffman made the remark, "Buzz, wouldn't it be great if we could get ahold of "der Fuehrer," stick one of those damn "screaming meemies" where the sun don't shine, and send him on his way?" "Damn right," I answered, "but that would be too good for him, as many lives as he has destroyed!"

General Patton's Third Army was advancing so fast, that our supply lines were just about outrun during the first week of September. Gasoline, which was badly needed for our armored spearheads, plus ammunition and other needed supplies were trucked over four hundred miles from Normandy to this advancing front, mainly on the Red Ball express highway. By the middle of September, due to lack of supplies, and heavy unexpected enemy resistance, our Third Army was put in a holding position west of the mighty Moselle.

Marshal Gerd von Rundstedt, using all available German forces at this time, had managed to halt the Third Army's advance west of the Moselle River in the Alsace-Lorraine Province of France! This situation was supposed to be only temporary, as supplies would be forthcoming, along with much needed replacements. On this wide front that reached from the First Army sector in the north to the Seventh Army in the south, our Third Army held fast. There was much shelling from both sides and cross-fire to deal with as we pulled off both combat and reconnaissance patrols in daylight and darkness. When the City of Nancy, France, was taken, September 15th, the people were ecstatic, as the last of the Nazi defenders were flushed out and marched off to makeshift prisoner encampments. The newly liberated French residents swamped us with bear hugs, kisses and vins along with champagne they had hidden for this occasion!

On a dark and stormy night around the first of October before we resumed our offensive, word reached us that an isolated group of German Wehrmecht was terrorizing a French village west of Nancy. Two squads of our platoon, which included Lieutenant Garcia, Hoffman and me, were dispatched there with two tanks. As the tanks halted outside the village, our squads hopped off and approached from two directions. After about an hour of standoff activity where they were pinned down by the rapid firing of our Thompson sub-machine guns in the barricade they had set up, they quickly surrendered as the two Sherman tanks approached. Most of the village people were women and children and we received a warm vibrant reception, topped off with food and vins in the village's two cafes. The French people really showed their genuine appreciation for their American liberators and we appreciated their cooperation, as well as their friendly attitudes. Our two squads, the tanks, along with the captured "Jerries," (who gave us no trouble) arrived back at our outfit before daylight with zero casualties.

My outfit was ordered back to the area of the fortress City of Metz when the offensive was resumed by the Third Army. This was a slow, costly battle as our supplies were very limited. Gasoline was at a premium and our supporting 105 mm Howitzers were only allowed to fire less than ten rounds each, daily. It rained damn nearly every day, a slow dreary rain that kept us slogging through mud up to our ankles. One evening Hoffman and I were walking cautiously toward the entrance of a recently captured pillbox when an 88 mm shell screamed in and exploded right between us. Miraculously we both survived this onslaught without a scratch but we were thrown bodily many yards apart by concussion! When I got up and helped Hoffman to his feet, he exclaimed, "Buzz, I know damn well now that every damn "Kraut" in the Wehrmacht has an 88 at his disposal!" "Yes, Hoff," I answered, "I will always be on the lookout for the sob who invented that damn weapon!"

The whole damn three to four months of the fighting along the Meuse River in the Lorraine Province of France was costly and a hell of a bloody ordeal. The Wehrmacht was throwing everything, including the kitchen sink at Patton's Third Army, because they wanted to keep this colorful armored genius west of the Moselle as long as possible. The Germans knew damn well that when Patton's Third crossed the Moselle, into their first line of defense (the Siegfried Line), that there would be no way to stem this mighty drive into their homeland.

General Patton was a tough leader but fair to his men who were bogged down in Lorraine. He arranged for those of us who were longest at the front to get passes for Nancy, Reims, and even Paris. The Military Police in these cities would stamp the pass on arrival and also on departure, to make sure one didn't stay over the limit of time allotted. The time periods of transportation to and from these cities didn't count on the passes, as it was accomplished by hitch-hiking mostly on Army vehicles using the roadways. Hoffman and I selected Reims, and we enjoyed it very much. In a time frame of forty-eight hours, we first visited a small cafe where wine flowed like water. Music was played by a young girl with an accordion who could only play "La Paloma, La Gollindrina," and "Estralita." In English these songs are, "The Dove, The Swallow," and "Little Star." This music was fantastic to the ears of soldiers who were used to the noise of screaming, exploding artillery and other hell of war! My buddy and I danced to this haunting music with some of the most beautiful mademoiselles in Reims and stayed the night in the homes of their families, who treated us royally.

These ladies enjoyed our company as well as we did theirs, and the following day we all went sight-seeing in this city, especially in some of the museums where priceless paintings still hung. The Nazis didn't have time to take all valuables with them when this city was taken so fast, so some of us did get to come back and see what was by-passed. After one more night in the little cafe enjoying the company of these wonderful French people, with their wine and beautiful music to dance by, it was time to return to camp. When we departed the following morning, some wonderful memories went with us as we returned to the hell of war at the front!

"Hoff," I asked, "how did you enjoy the vacation in Reims? I think that neither hell nor high water could have made me leave that fabulous city in another time!" "You are damn right, Buzz," answered Hoffman, "I've a good mind to go back AWOL, if I thought it would work, but it wouldn't. Anyway, as you know, I have lots of revenge to catch up on!" "Yes, I know my friend, and I am here to help you do so!" I replied in no uncertain manner. "We make one hell of a team, Buzz," Hoff spoke out as we picked up our weapons and took our places on the edge of "no man's land." Mail call this day brought no word from Annie in Italy and I don't believe she has survived.

Without forthcoming supplies, the Third Army had no other alterative but to hold the line along the formidable Meuse River. Once across this River, the advance was slow mostly due to supplies which were still very short. The month of October passed with bitter fighting to bring our front closer to the Moselle. The damn fall rains kept four to five inches of mud on the terrain and with heavy German resistance, the Rhine, our goal, seemed to be further away, as all high ground and villages became harder and bloodier to conquer. From the first week in November until the second week in December, the Third Army had advanced approximately forty miles. The last fort in the Metz area of the Maginot Line was captured at this time, after flushing out the last Nazis that held these strategic positions. All of these fortresses were connected by underground tunnels with a railroad track connecting each one with the other. These fortresses were underground and that made it pure hell to clear them of the enemy. The General was seen walking through one of these fortresses one day and in the dim light saw a soldier over in a corner. He then stopped, asked the soldier what he was doing and was told that he was taking a leak. After telling the soldier that he was the only sob that knew what he was doing, he continued on his way. The fall of Metz took place at this time and the Moselle River was finally crossed by the Third Army after one hell of a bloody battle. The way was now cleared for a fast race of Patton's armored spearheads through the Siegfried Line to the formidable Rhine. This move, however, was not to be at this time, due to circumstances beyond control.

It was now December 16, 1944, and the Battle of the Bulge was in its beginning stage, so a vast lid was put on all plans for the time being. My outfit would soon be heading for the snow-covered Ardennes to help stem this mad Nazi drive to reach the vital allied seaport of Antwerp, Belgium. Orders to move out would soon be announced by General Patton!

One thing is certain about life in an infantry outfit in combat, and that is the fact that you are like a rolling stone. You keep moving until you are stopped by the enemy and if it is impossible for you to move on, you dig in. The noble pick-mattock shovel is used to dig a shallow trench or foxhole in order to afford yourself minimum protection from bullets and bursting shells. There are times when you may find an empty root cellar or farmhouse basement, after making sure there are no bobby trap wires to trip. Most of the time you are in the open, regardless of weather conditions or enemy fire. There were three combat commands in my armored infantry battalion: Combat Command A, Combat Command B, and Combat Command R. CCA and CCB would be on the front lines, and CCR would be in reserve, and would move up after getting replacements or whatever else behind the lines to accomplish. Then CCA or CCB would have a turn at CCR, we rotated when in a holding position, otherwise all would be on the line in an attack offensive.

Now on December 20th, riding on tanks and half-tracks, my outfit had 75 miles to go through snow, ice and temperatures around and below zero. Our objective was to attack at the besieged Belgium city of Bastogne and relieve General McAuliffe's 101 Airborne Division who were surrounded by Elite Nazi forces. Wish us luck!

To stop the Third Army's advance into the Saarland and hence the Seigfried Line, where we would make a fast drive to the Rhine, was a real kick in the backend for this outfit. Since the Nazi's last big shot was by breaking through our First Army defenses, it was damn necessary that we help stem this drive first by all means available. That is the very reason we were braving the terrible winter elements. In this snow, icy roads totally covered and 20 degrees below zero weather temperature, our spearhead moved through Luxembourg to make contact with the Nazi armies surrounding Bastogne, and open up a corridor to the city. We knew this would be one hell of a job, but with tanks, infantry, and lots of fire power, we could damn well do it or die trying! The roads were so invisible, due to the heavy snow and drifts, that the half-tracks Hoffman and I were riding on nearly went over a cliff. I do know for a fact that all of our group was hoping and praying that the 101 Airborne would be able to hold out for the time it would take us to open up a passage into Bastogne. It was getting close to Christmas, but it was far, far away this year. "I know damn well I am freezing, Hoffman," I spoke up, "because I don't have any feeling in my legs and feet." "Perk up, Buzz," was his reply, "I have none from my waist down." About that time the vehicle stopped to let us get off and stomp our feet (to help circulation) some before continuing onward. Again, we ask and pray for good luck, as we will really need it. Also we need the wintry skies to clear!

Chapter 8
The Battle of the Bulge

At 0200 hours in the morning of December 16, 1944, the greatest land battle of World War II began to materialize. Nazi hordes (under command of Field Marshall General Karl Rudolph Gerd von Rundstedt) roared out of the snow, ice and freezing fog of the formidable Ardennes hills and forests of Belgium. There were nineteen Wehrmacht and nine SS Panzer divisions, twenty-eight divisions total, that broke through the thin lines of the United States First Army. Their mission, to reach and take-over the crucial Allied seaport of Antwerp. These Nazi hordes were using the "scorched earth" policy like a wounded dragon in its last throws, leaving a trail of death and destruction in its bloody path. Their giant Panzers (tanks), as well as their infantry and artillery, especially their 88 mm, were tearing one hell of a hole in the Allied defenses.

My outfit was pulled out of our drive from the Saar into the Seigfried Line where General Patton's race to the Rhine was called off temporarily. This enemy counter offensive must be stopped at all costs, so every combat command available was needed to bring it to a halt. This Nazi assault through the Ardennes threatened to overrun everything in its path and reach the Meuse within several days.

Our Third Army of a quarter million men plus thousands of tanks, trucks, and other vehicles, on December 20th, tackled the icy, snow-covered roads leading to our objective, Bastogne, Belgium. The hard pressed surrounded 101 Airborne division was holding this besieged city at all costs, as General McAuliffe, its commander had already said "nuts" to Field Marshall von Runstedt's note demanding his surrender!

Hoffman, who was at my side on this hazardous move toward Bastogne spoke out, "Buzz, I'm damn nearly frozen now, and when our destination is reached, I am sure as hell we will attack at once, because if we don't, we are all going to be frozen stiff!" My reply to this was, "Hoff, it is snowing like hell now, the temperature is near zero, and it's going to stay this way. Bastogne is snowed in, and surrounded by the "Jerries," so there is no doubt that we will attack on arrival!"

We were not too well prepared, clothing-wise, as our overcoats were too damn bulky; however, our dark green combat jackets allowed us to move more freely. Also, most of us had wool caps under our helmets, a warm wool GI sweater, and long johns. Our combat boots were not waterproof as snow seeped through the leather even though most of us had treated them with a damn pound of dubbin! Our socks would get wet through the boots, causing them to freeze, and bring about "frozen feet" or "trench foot." To help this situation, we carried an extra pair of socks to change, when possible, and the wet ones were put over each shoulder, under our jackets to dry with body heat. Anyway, what we had in the way of combat attire, under these extreme weather conditions, we made the best of without a lot of bitching!

Our armored spearhead, heading north through Luxembourg would attack the southern reaches of the "bulge", ever widening with the flow of Nazi forces. When we stopped off in a small Luxembourg town on December 21st to make a minor repair to the half-track my squad was riding on, in support of the tanks, we were pleasantly surprised. A young lady, accompanied by an elderly couple came out of an old shelled-out building, into the snow-covered roadway with a large pot of steaming coffee. This was like a sign from heaven to a squad of half-frozen infantrymen. As she poured the coffee into our canteen cups, she spoke in fluent English, this is not very much, but it is all we have to offer. We wish you the best in the great battle ahead and may you be blessed by the Gracious Virgin." "Thank you for your kindness," was my reply, as we moved on, momentarily, into the snowy void. The coffee was imitation, and was most likely left by "Jerry," in his retreat from this area, but it really soothed and warmed this bunch of GI Joes who would soon be in mortal combat.

On the morning of December 22nd our Third Army attacked the Nazi perimeter around Bastogne on a twenty-mile front. As forecasted, it snowed all day with no let up, as our infantry, tanks, artillery and other units advanced at least six miles over this ice and snow covered Ardennes terrain. Thanks to our artillery whose powerful 105 howitzers pounded the hell out of enemy positions, so our infantry and tanks could advance slowly, but surely, against this fanatic enemy. This battle to bring relief to Bastogne was violently intense, as we were fighting much of the "Elite Troopen SS," and several Nazi Panzer Grenadier divisions, along with Colonel Remer's fanatical SS brigade which reaked much havoc. We had no air support due to the snow and freezing fog that kept an impenetrable blanket over this entire operation!

As darkness descended upon us, intense fire raked our positions from the enemies machine guns, 120 mm mortars and the merciless 88 mm artillery. Digging in was pure hell as the terrain was block frozen. The only way a shallow trench or foxhole could be dug was to wait for a shell to explode, then dig where it tore into the earth, that is if you survived the bombardment.

Lieutenant Garcia, Hoffman and I had been together for quite awhile and I had been wondering if our luck would hold, as we all had many close encounters with enemy fire. This particular night the Lieutenant, Hoffman, and I went on reconnaissance patrol with several of our replacements, as hardly any of the old timers were left. Our helmets were whitewashed and with white long johns over our clothing, we set out into "no man's land" to find out what lay ahead. There were many dead and frozen Nazi soldiers along the way, but we finally reached an area that bristled with gun emplacements and tanks. This was a very dangerous mission, during which time as I was lying in fir brush viewing this stronghold, a hobnail boot made an imprint on my left hand. That was close, but my hand was almost frozen and didn't have much feeling in it anyway. We returned to our lines before daylight safe, but half frozen. Our recon patrol was very successful, as the stronghold ahead that we located, was zeroed in by our artillery (whispering death), and knocked out!

The second day showed no signs of clearing, so we made some headway, still under intense fire that the enemy was unceasingly throwing at us. In the Ardennes forest we really caught hell, and many casualties from short fused 88 mm shells exploding at treetop level, sending deadly shrapnel in all directions to the ground level. These were the deadly "tree bursts" or "star bursts" that would get you as you lay flat on the earth or in trenches or foxholes, there was no way to get away from them. Many casualties took place in these forests where the trees were actually torn to hell! The advance continued slowly with very intense enemy fire, along with ice, snow, and bitter cold. Finally Christmas Eve and Day came and went as we nibbled on "K" rations up front and pushed further an armored wedge in the enemy's lines before Bastogne. Every soldier in the Third Army received a Christmas card from General Patton. There was a Merry Christmas wish on one side, and on the other was a prayer asking for good weather and victory. This was a great uplift of morale, especially for an army in mortal combat with a fanatic enemy, just to know their Commanding General is much concerned about their well being. Patton was a fabulous Field General and the front lines were no stranger to him! He was seen many times at the front under heavy fire from the Nazis, and I believe he was definitely without fear.

Finally, after four days of fierce fighting, our spearhead made contact with the 101 Airborne division, the battered bastards of Bastogne. This contact took place on December 26th, just before the miserable, snow-blanketed, and freezing night fell upon the devastated Belgium countryside. Just one look at this told the whole story of the gallant troops who held it under the extreme conditions created by mother nature and the mortal storms. There was not one building that wasn't damaged grotesquely or completely destroyed. Many of the better buildings of stone or brick that were not destroyed were showing wide cracks from shell concussion with the outer walls sprayed with shrapnel and machine gun fire. What a hell of a mess! After a night of intense enemy fire from 88 mm artillery, screaming meemies, 120 mm mortars and machine guns, we broadened our advance into Bastogne, pushing the "Jerries" back on both sides. Soon after daylight, the wounded were being evacuated, and much-needed supplies were being brought into this long besieged city!

Breaking the siege of Bastogne was one of the greatest feats of World War II. It took General Patton's Third Army to do it and so it was done with much sacrifice by an army of brave men! I do not know how in the hell we did it, but Hoffman, Lieutenant Garcia, and I stayed together in our combat team without becoming casualties since Normandy, and that feat in itself was almost unbelievable. We were the only three who were left in our original Platoon, and for us, it was continuously "one day at a time!" It is almost impossible for anyone in combat to go through the hell of war for months on end without becoming some sort of casualty. But here we were, and realized a great victory over the evil Third Reich was in the foreseeable future once the Third Army's drive to the Rhine could resume! Our great General Patton and every soldier on this vital front wished for and prayed for the skies to open up and overpower this wintry blast that had kept us at bay for so long a period. Our Air Force was badly needed to soften up this well-prepared Nazi drive, so our great army could begin the advance that would forever vanquish this evil from the face of civilization!

As late evening of December 27th rolled around in this city still under bombardment, our squad just returning from a combat patrol in enemy lines, received some hot food for the first time in many days. A temporary field kitchen had been set up in the basement of a bombed-out building and a staggered chow line was forming. Hoffman and Garcia yelled out, "Buzz, we now are all going to get a damn hot meal, we are going to get a new sleeping bag and we can sleep for six whole hours in the basement where they have a makeshift stove with real fire set up!" My answer was, "Hoff, Garcia, is the damn world coming to an end? This is too good to be true, maybe we get to wash up and shave." "You damn right," said Garcia, "but we all got to relieve the front line outpost in the wee hours, so enjoy!" We did enjoy this fresh up and rest, after indulging in a meal of fried Spam, dehydrated potatoes and peas, along with hot java that was so strong it could actually walk. Garcia had a bottle of cognac which he shared with us all and its warmth could be felt clean down to the damn near frozen toes! After taking a "spit bath" in water warmed in our helmets, we changed socks, wrote a letter home by the light attached to our tank's generator, then hit the sack on the concrete floor in our new sleeping bags. Heaven at last!

Called from a deep sleep at 0200 hours, Hoffman and I took our places at the outpost on the edge of "no man's land," relieving our two buddies, who also needed a rest. The 88 mm shells were still coming in and the chatter of Nazi machine guns was prevalent, but our two-man concrete reinforced guard post offered minimum protection from direct hits. During these trying times of this Battle of the Bulge, Nazi spies dressed in American uniforms, speaking fluent English, were infiltrating our ranks, creating havoc, much confusion and sabotaging whenever possible. Every GI you met and didn't know offhand had to be checked out with trick questions, and have knowledge of the daily "password."

This early snowy morning of December 28th, "Axis Sally" came in on a nearby Sherman tank's radio. "Hi guys, hope you are having a great time! Your wives and sweethearts surely are, back home with the four-Fs." After a record played with instrumental and a female singer with a beautiful vocal of "Lilli Marlene," Sally signed off with "Remember boys, the password is artillery barrage and are you damn well going to get it!" This had been our "password" and 88 mm artillery opened up like a door to hell in minutes! So it turned out that our ranks were so infiltrated with the enemy in GI uniforms that there seemed to be no way to keep military secrets of tight security. The enemy seemed to know our every move in advance, which was absolutely devastating to our morale! General Patton was mad as hell and our Supreme Commander even had a "double" (an Army Colonel) ride in his car to headquarters in Versailles each day during this crisis.

Advancing to and liberating Bastogne was a great feat in itself, but the weather was cold, snow was deep and the damn war was far from over. The enemy was still fighting hard, their self-propelled artillery was on the minus side, along with hundreds of Tiger-Panther tanks, but they seemed very determined to fight against all odds. Even some of their big guns were moved into position by horses! This was a damn shame because one of the saddest things I saw during these trying times were shell-shocked horses wandering aimlessly around in "no man's land."

After reaching the outskirts of Bastogne, my outfit advanced slowly eastward against tough enemy opposition. One evening, the snow stopped and my squad, working with two Sherman tanks, witnessed a beautiful red sunset in this land of ice and snow close-by the Luxembourg border. At the time we were just behind the front, regrouping new replacements for our casualty losses. Just before reaching a shelled-out farmhouse where temporary company headquarters would be set up, we came across three young girls sparsely dressed and damn nearly frozen. Naturally, we took them with us to the farmhouse (where after checking for booby traps) a small fire was started for warmth and heating up Nescafe along with "C" rations. The girls were Belgian but spoke German in that area, so after a warm up and hot rations, they told us why they were alone in this desolate place. First, they took off kerchiefs showing their plight of completely shaved heads. Their villagers had shaved off these young girls hair and ostracized them from their homes, sending them out in this frozen wilderness probably to freeze to death. Their crime was that they had been overly friendly with the Nazis, their punishment was mandatory, regardless of the reasons or legitimate excuses, such as even the threat of death if they had refused these "swinehund!" War is really hell for the soldier, also the people who are exposed to the ravages of it. War changes the lives of all who experience this storm, created by mortals who destroy civilization in more ways than any other malady. Thanks be to the gracious God for the end of this Nazi tyranny and victory for the Allied liberators!

This shell-damaged farmhouse served as our company headquarters for three days, while we regrouped and rested. While there, we got to wash up, enjoy heated Nescafe with "C" rations, and have an electric light with power from one of our tank's generators to read and write, the first time in many days. Also the young Belgian girls, turned over to the Red Cross, would be joining other displaced persons, driven from their homes and families in this devastating war.

Back on the front our advance was in a slow moving position, due to terrible weather and a ruthless enemy, now with nothing to lose. The Nazis were fighting unmercifully to hold out with all odds against them, but we gave them hell, as our armored and infantry penetrated deeper into their defenses, regardless of the weather, which made the Ardennes terrain all but impassable.

New Year's Day came and left, but not without a Happy New Year 1945 wish-and-pep talk to boost these hard fighting front liners of the Third Army, from none other than General Patton himself. This Ardennes battle was still an intense and bloody campaign which lasted for days, bringing many casualties to both sides. Bastogne was still under attack by the hard-line Nazis, both Wehrmacht, and SS Panzer grenadiers. This was an all out assault by these fanatical Nazis, to take back what we had conquered, but they damn well were not going to succeed as we would see to that. Lieutenant Garcia became a casualty in this battle.

The weather definitely would not cooperate, as it would snow, thaw at times, then everything would freeze over again. However, our tanks and infantry held, sometimes under terrific odds, while our "whispering death" artillery pounded the hell out of the "Jerries." On clear days (which were few and far between) sometimes our P-47 and P-51 fighter planes gave us much-needed support.

One cold snowy morning around the middle of January, my squad returning from a combat patrol, was ambushed. We split up and went in different directions as none of us were about to surrender to these fanatics, not after the Malmedy Massacre by Colonel Peiper's combat team of the First SS Panzer division! Taking cover behind a stone wall, Hoffman and I were catching our breath when all at once he whispered to me, "Buzz, don't look now, but I can hear German language being spoken close-by." I did look up and there was the barrel of an 88 mm gun right over my head. "Hoffman," I said in a whisper, "that is the gun of a 72-ton King Tiger Panzer, which is right on the other side of this wall. Let's split up and get behind him." With bazooka and rockets, we managed to reach a wooded area behind this monster. With Hoffman as my assistant who loaded and wired the rocket, I fired one which knocked out one weak spot (engine) and another that knocked off part of a track. Believe me, those damn Nazis came out of that smoking tank with hands over their helmets yelling "comrade!" They had been had, so without much coaxing, these prisoners were taken back to our lines where we turned them in for processing in the POW enclosures. In a few days the greatest land battle of World War II was just about over. The Battle of the Bulge ended on January 25, 1945, with Allied casualties amounting to a whopping 89,000 of which 19,000 were killed in action! The Nazi army had lost many more, 120,000 casualties and 600 tanks! Not even a tree in the Ardennes forests was left without heavy damage!

May man never have to fight a campaign again, such as this crucial Battle of the Bulge, in the formidable Ardennes. May the gracious God bless all who fought and died in this battle which was the turning point for the liberators of the enslaved countries of

Europe! Now, the Third Army's advance to the distant Rhine would proceed, after breaching Germany's west wall, the formidable Siegfried Line! May the Lord be with us on this mighty mission.

I steadfastly believe that the Lord was with us, as the liberators who would vanquish an evil so vast, that it had left a trail of death and destruction over endless boundaries. As our Third Army advanced into this formidable West Wall, the thought of complete victory was on everyone's mind. It would be a vast undertaking, and there would be many more casualties, but courage, determination and faith, throughout history has always won over evil and deception! Also, we had admiration for the most colorful General in the United States Army, who thought enough of his men to give them a card of faith for Christmas. Even though my presents and cards from home didn't arrive on the front, that card was a real morale booster! May the All Supreme be ever with these brave soldiers of General Patton's Third Army!

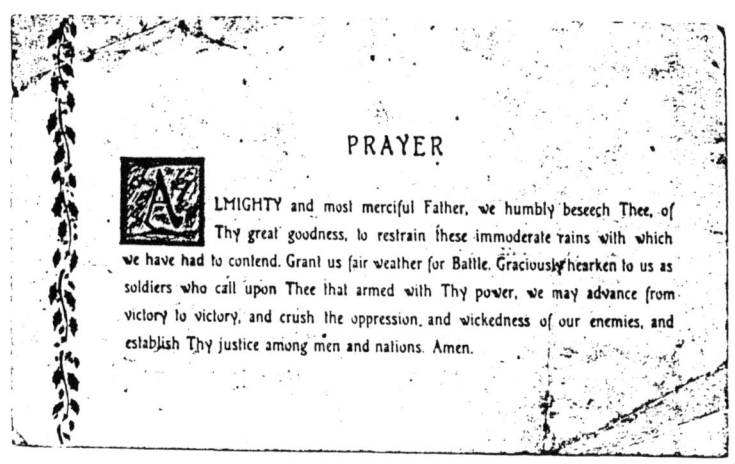

General Patton's famous prayer for the Third Army in Lorraine, France.

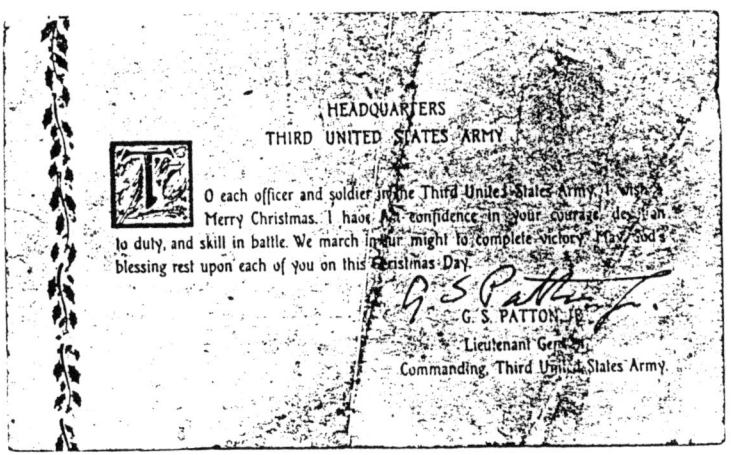

Every soldier in General Patton's Third Army received a *Merry Christmas* greeting during the decisive Battle of the Bulge.

Chapter 9
Through the Siegfried Line to the Rhine

With the Battle of the Bulge now contained and won, our Third Army was once more on the move, into the Deutschland. The once ferocious Nazi Dragon was now in its last throes, but still very determined to keep General Patton's army out of the formidable Siegfried Line and Rhineland!

During the great snows, our tanks and other vehicles were whitewashed, then after a thaw, we all had to pitch in and wash off the damn white in the freezing waters of small rivers and streams! This, along with fighting a fanatic enemy was enough to send a good combat soldier in search of a Section Eight (psycho-discharge). Our advance was still slow toward the east, and the weather continued bad. Snow, thaw, freeze, then if not these three hazards, there was the eternal mud that bogged down both man and vehicle. All of this was enough to knock hell out of a doughboy's morale, but with determination for victory, we pushed on through hell and high water. Each night "bed check Charley" (Nazi recon plane) would make his droning rounds, sometimes turning loose a phosphorus bomb. This phosphorus would spread its white hot particles in all directions, and if hit, one would have to remove the burning particle with a sharp instrument. If it wasn't removed fast, the phosphorus would burn to the bone or more. I have a deep scar on my right leg as a result of such a burn although it has been there for over 50 years.

I can remember a time during the heavy snows when my squad was on recon patrol in a large Belgian town close-by the German border. I am sure we had been spotted by Nazi soldiers who still held this town, so we took cover in a snowbank. We were damn nearly frozen when it was decided the coast was clear, so out we crawled one by one. We didn't know which way to go as it was snowing again very hard. As we got our bearings and headed toward the cover of some buildings, a cathedral loomed through the now blizzard. An English-speaking Catholic priest and six French nuns who had been watching our plight through their darkened windows by the light of enemy flares, called us into a basement door. We were freezing cold, but didn't go in at once, not until we were sure. They came out and helped two of us in, as the rest were able to walk. In that basement, there was a candlelight in the room which was warmed with a small coal heater. These wonderful people had rescued this nearly frozen group of combat Americans from right under the Nazis' noses. After a warm-up, some hot barley soup, and a glass of brandy, we said our thanks and farewell, and with renewed vigor made it safely back to our lines.

All of the people of eastern Belgium were extra nice to us, as many nights when we were in a defensive position, they invited us to sleep in their homes, treating us as part of the family. As I remember, it was cold as hell during these times and any shelter was a welcome sight. Many times we slept with the cattle in the barn addition to their homes. In these times everyone took turns in guarding the area. On these cold snowy nights we would stand in the shadow of the tanks on the ravaged streets, in our sleeping bags, to keep from freezing. The zipper would be open and our trusty M-1 rifles would be held in readiness. Our now larger M-26 Pershing tanks with the 90 mm gun was a big change from the smaller Shermans. From the generators on these tanks came the power to light one room, which would be blacked out in these situations. We always shared our food with these friendly Belgians who spoke German, this close to Germany's border. Sometimes a field kitchen would be set up and all food leftovers were given to them and the children. Also, our cigarettes were shared with the grown-ups, and chewing gum with the wonderful children. Their friendliness and consideration helped our morale, and the small amounts of wines and cognac they shared warmed our very being. During these times enemy shells never ceased coming in.

These were the times our battalion would revert from front line Combat Commands A or B to Combat Command R (reserve), to regroup and fill in our casualty ranks with fresh replacements. This would afford the only chance we would have to shave, clean up and get some much needed hot food and rest. Back on the line in a couple of days, we would be slugging it out again with the enemy, pushing him ever closer toward "unconditional surrender!"

After the fall of St. Vith, the spearhead of which my outfit was a part, pushed into the outskirts of the sprawling town of Prum, Germany, along the River Prum. There was a lot of resistance to cope with from these fanatic Nazis and their 88 artillery had us zeroed in, virtually pinned down. We finally decided that they must have a forward observer in a tall church steeple directing fire. Calling for a few rounds of "whispering death" from our 155 mm artillery, the ancient steeple disappeared, the 88 mm shells began exploding off target, and Prum was conquered the following day. Of course, there was the clean-up operation to go through, from street to street and house to house, as with all cities, towns or villages in this war against the Nazis in their homeland. In France we had help from the Marquis and Free French, but here in the Deutschland everyone was a potential enemy and was treated as such. General Patton put out a "no fraternization"order, and it was abided by for a time, but it didn't hold up, because questions came up that had to be answered either in English or German.

Soon after the conquest of Prum, we advanced, under heavy enemy resistance, to a forested area where our line of defense was set up for the night. Hoffman, six others and I went out on combat recon patrol during this moonless night to find out what lay ahead to cope with on the morrow. What we discovered was a concentration of Panther and Tiger tanks, a battery of 88 mm artillery, actually part of a damn SS Panzer division in readiness to counter attack, at the first sign of our movement. Hoffman whispered to me, "Buzz, do you see what the hell is waiting to ambush our outfit when we go into the attack tomorrow?" "Yes, Hoffman, you damn well right I see it and that is why we have to get back pronto and warn headquarters!" After planting plastic explosives on several of the camouflaged tank's tracks, then we crawled silently through "no man's land" after leaving the enemy stronghold. Upon reaching our Company Command post, which was in a log dugout taken from the enemy during the past day, we filled the captain in on our recon patrol discovery. In turn, the chain of command went into action, and in a short order, forward observers came up to direct artillery fire on the enemy's location. Within minutes, "outgoing mail," projectiles from our 105 mm, 155 mm, and 240 mm guns began their "whispering death" blitz of this stronghold, just west of Germany's West Wall. The whisper of these projectiles passing over our heads and exploding in the Nazi's position was music to our ears, throughout this long night! We received some "incoming mail" from the enemy's 88 mm artillery, but it only lasted for several hours, then all was silent as our "whispering death" onslaught continued on, until long after first light.

When our infantry and tanks attacked before noon, we encountered quite a few rounds of 88 mm shells, along with volley after volley of "screaming meemies" being fired from a high ridge to our left flank. The M-26 Pershing tank to which Hoffman and I were clinging, turned its 90 mm gun toward the ridge, fired twice, then all was silent for the moment. In a few minutes our squad jumped off the two M-26 tanks, and followed by the rest of the soldiers in our platoon, made our way through a small village which had been evacuated by civilians. The few Wehrmacht soldiers still holding out soon surrendered, and our men advanced on a thawing, muddy road which led to the first row of "dragon's teeth" (concrete tank barriers) in the German West Wall (Siegfried Line). In staggered formation we advanced unopposed, but in a few minutes all of hell broke loose! Machine-gun fire raked our ranks, and more "screaming meemie" rockets zeroed in, as we took cover the best we could on this open road. I hit a snow-covered ditch and promptly broke the thin coat of ice below, getting soaked from the waist down. I had my M-1 rifle and the bazooka, Hoffman behind me had his M-1 and six bazooka rockets. With M-26 tanks covering us, we were able to quiet one machine gun nest and a "screaming meemie" launching site! Our medics were very busy as there were many casualties on this open road that offered little cover. Just before the "dragon's teeth," were several burned out Tiger tanks and a Mercedes-Benz automobile with two dead and frozen Nazi SS officers, one inside, the other lying across the hood. The night before had been bitter cold and several more Nazis frozen in death were passed along the way. Moving through the first row of "dragon's teeth" one of our replacements went berserk and was holding onto one of the "dragon's teeth" for dear life, so one of the medics gave him a shot, then he was evacuated. Another round of 88 mm artillery hit us, along with machine-gun fire, which one of our bazooka rockets silenced. It was now getting dark and colder than hell, because my wet clothes were freezing to my body. The Nazis at this time had the high ground and we had the low ground, so the order was to dig in for the night. As a pillbox to our left was blown apart from 240 mm shelling the night before, Hoffman and the rest of my squad (including me) took cover in this topless reinforced concrete shambles. We didn't even have a K ration that night.

Our squad later went out on recon patrol, made it back, then dug foxholes forward of the pillbox ruins, which were being torn apart by 88 mm "incoming mail" from the enemy. Digging in with our pick-mattocks shovels wasn't too hard, because we dug where 88s had torn holes in the frozen earth. Somehow my body heat had dried the icy moisture in my clothing during the night's activity, and when daylight came, I could move more freely, feeling quite comfortable. This day my outfit just held on to what territory we had, because the enemy was shelling the hell out of our positions, and also we needed many replacements. As evening rolled around we had managed to capture a concrete reinforced pillbox intact, so Company headquarters was set up in it. As darkness fell, 88 mm shells began a real barrage all around and on this recessed pillbox. Hoffman and I were in the two-man guard post with built-up concrete sides to the right of this pillbox standing guard, when a strange thing took place. A Wehrmacht captain walked up from the nearby hedgerow with hands over his helmet calling out "comrade!" The full moon was shining, so we could see his every move. I asked, "Vas ist, captain?" His answer in plain English was, "I would like to surrender myself and my company, what is left of it, so please take me to your leader." After confiscating his Luger and ammo, I escorted him into the pillbox, turning him over to our captain. In a few minutes, my squad escorted him to where the remnants of a cold and hungry company was waiting, then escorted them back to headquarters where they were marched to the rear as POWs. Some of the guys expected a trap, but it didn't happen, as this officer seemed very determined in his decision and stated that he knew the war was lost, and wished to surrender to Americans than to the Russians!

All of the following day, "incoming mail," 88s and "screaming meemies," along with 120 mm mortars, hampered our every move. Toward evening, however, the freezing fog that blanketed this whole area lifted, revealing blue sky and sunshine. The Air Force fighters were then called in and they dive-bombed, then strafed the Krauts ahead with their 50 caliber machine guns. Two of these planes, P-51 Mustangs were shot down over the enemy lines, but the pilots bailed out, and were rescued by one of our combat patrols in a short order. The planes had softened up the German defenses ahead, and at any time now we could advance with "minimum" instead of "maximum" casualties.

Going out on recon patrol that night, it was a full moon, so we had to move very slow and quietly through the Nazi defenses, which actually were in shambles now. Returning at midnight Hoffman and I reported our find, then hit the guard post again for two hours, afterward a break to rest inside the German bunker. The 88 projectiles continued on through the night and early morning hours, and one came right between Hoffman and me just before we entered the bunker's recessed door. That same night, we received a GI can full of coffee that was block frozen, and which was accompanied by doughnuts so damn hard that they could have been used for weapons. However, this was appreciated very much as we melted the coffee, piece by piece, and dunked the doughnuts. Thanks to the Red Cross, as it took time to get these goodies to the front and they went very well with the eternal "K" rations.

The following morning, after a breakfast "K" ration, our battalion along with an M-26 tank battalion jumped off into an attack to secure the high ground from the enemy in this pillbox-laden West Wall. The going was rough, but the advance was going along successfully. Our artillery shells would not penetrate the reinforced walls of the steel and concrete of the West Wall bunkers, so the only way they could be taken was by infantry. The recessed steel doors were blown off by dynamite, then grenades were tossed in. The enemy would then come out, that is, those who were able to do so. This day during the evening hours as my platoon had almost reached the high ground, a volley of "screaming meemies" accompanied by some 88 projectiles exploded among us, leaving many casualties.

As if these damn enemy projectiles were not enough, the Luftwaffe, which had been hiding out for some time, due to lack of planes and fuel, showed up in more force than we had seen until now. First a lone Stuka dive bomber coming in close, let go a bomb that knocked out one of our M-26 tanks, setting it and a half-track on fire, causing many casualties. When the Stuka pulled out of this dive, gaining altitude, it was hit by a 90 mm projectile from another M-26 tank of ours, then went down in a trail of black smoke, crashing and exploding over the ridge. Within minutes, our column was straffed by two ME-109s followed by a Ju-88. Shortly thereafter, this show of the Luftwaffe was broken up by two of our Air Force P-47 Thunderbolts, and a British Spitfire. Then two P-51 Mustangs began dive-bombing targets ahead of our spearhead.

As everything seemed to be quieting a little, all at once a volley of those awful sounding "screaming meemies," along with a number of 88 projectiles came in, exploded, and blasted the hell out of us. Our medics really were kept busy, as there were many casualties. I had concussion, and my right leg had no feeling from thigh to foot. For now I was out of it, as I was diagnosed with these sustained injuries at the evacuation hospital behind the front. It was now February of 1945, I believed that victory was just over the horizon, and I damned well wanted to get back to the front and help bring it about!

Chapter 10
From Battle Casualty and Back to Combat

From the evacuation hospital, I was sent to a field hospital, then to a general hospital at St. Denis, France. At this United States Army operated hospital close-by the jewel of France, Paris, I was diagnosed with concussion, battle fatigue and physical exhaustion. My height was 6 feet and I had dropped in weight from 165 to 130 pounds soaking wet! After being checked out most of the evening of arrival with a series of x-rays, and examinations by army medical specialists, I was assigned to a semi-private room for treatment. When someone has been through the hell of battle for many weeks without sleep, and is also under the strain of severe concussion, the nervous system is so shattered, that normal sleep is impossible. That was my condition, along with a ruptured ear drum and numbness from the right thigh to knee. When the orderlies moved me from the wheelchair to the hospital bed in the assigned room, a First Lieutenant in the Nurses Corps gave me a shot that put me into a deep sleep almost immediately.

The following morning, when I awoke, the First Lieutenant nurse was at my bedside with all of her equipment. "How is the combat infantryman doing this morning?" she asked. "Not too good," I said, "but much better after the first good night's sleep in months! My darn head is throbbing and my ears are ringing like the "Blue Bells of Scotland!" All at once a familiar male voice spoke out, "Nurse, that can be only a combat soldier in my platoon who was at my side from Normandy to the Ardennes. "Hi, Buzz, how are things at the front? Is Hoffman still with the outfit?" I couldn't hear very well, but I did recognize the voice of Lieutenant Garcia, so I answered, "Lieutenant, how glad I am that you are alive, I should have known that the damn Krauts couldn't kill a legend. Yes, our buddy, Hoffman, is still slugging it out up front with a vengeance! I got it in the Siegfried Line, but I hope to get back to the Third Army before the Rhine crossing." His reply was, "you damn right, Buzz, you and myself also, we got to get the hell back and make history again. My wound has about healed, but the concussion is slower, anyway I am getting there!"

Just at this time, a French nurses aide brought breakfast in. Garcia jumped into his with vigor, but I couldn't eat a damn thing without throwing it back up, not even the coffee. Later, the nurse on duty came in before lunch, gave me a shot, and when the food arrived, I was able to eat and hold down a portion of it. The rest of this day was a series of memory lapses due to my concussion, and heavy medication. When the French lady brought in our evening meal, I may have eaten half of it before I passed out. Later, the nurse gave me a shot in the butt which put me to sleep for at least twelve hours.

When I awoke, Lieutenant Garcia was sitting up in a chair reading *The African Queen*. "Damn, Lieutenant Garcia," I said, "don't you go and try to beat me out of this hospital. We must leave together, so as to get in there, finish this damn war, and reap the harvest of victory!" "Don't worry, Buzz," replied Garcia, "I still have some time to go yet before I will be released from the hospital. I am also hoping we can leave here together for the big victory drive which I know will take place once the Third Army crosses the Rhine." "By the way," Lieutenant Garcia added, "who was my replacement when I became a casualty?" "Well, Lieutenant Garcia, to this question I have a damn good answer, Platoon Sergeant Jones who had the full cooperation of the whole platoon, even though they were mostly replacements, they fought like hell in that battle. Sergeant Jones led the platoon for the next forty-eight hours, then was relieved by a Lieutenant Harrison who was sent from headquarters. I really think Jones should have been commissioned a Second Lieutenant on the battlefield!" "Absolutely, Buzz," put in Garcia, "Jones is a damn good leader and a battlefield commission should have gone to him and next to him, you or Hoffman! How in the hell do we read the minds of the upper crust?" At this time, the nurse came in, gave me some pain medication and a shot of insulin. "This, soldier," she said, "will help your appetite, and get your body back to normal."

What the nurse said sounded good, but I knew that I had a hell of a long way to go. I did manage to hold down my breakfast for the first time, so that was a big move forward. After breakfast, I managed to take a long nap, and when I awoke, one of the French nurses aides who called herself "Madame Shu-Shu" was bringing in lunch. "Monsieur Buzz," she asked, "you like to have ze lunch now zat Madame Shu-Shu bring for you?" "What is on the menu

Madame," I asked. "It is soup du jour, music soup (bean), and zat you get gelatin and fruit cocktail, no much! Ze Lieutenant Garcia is go to ze cafeteria in ze wheelchair." The lunch was light and so was I, very lightheaded! Even when I got up to go to the latrine, I was very dizzy.

Every day Madame Shu-Shu brought me three light meals for the first week and each day the nurse gave me a shot of insulin. By the end of the week, Garcia and I were both going to the big mess hall at the end of a long outside concrete walk, in our wheelchairs. I was still having beaucoup dizzy spells, my headaches would come and go, and my ears continued to ring, but I was improving. The numbness in my right thigh was better, and the main cause of that problem proved to be overexposure to the snow and freezing weather conditions for long periods of time.

Madame Shu-Shu came to see Lieutenant Garcia and me every day, and she had quite a lot to talk about. One day when she was cleaning the room, a cute little nurse came in and gave me a shot. When she left, I made the remark, "Garcia, that one is a real beauty, and attractive, I sure would like to take her out!" Garcia agreed, and Madame Shu-Shu spoke up, "Remember Monsieur Buzz, all zat glitter is no gold!" She was quite a girl, Madame Shu-Shu, probably in her 60s. The older lady who sometimes worked with her was a card also, even though she spoke little English. "Gritty Gertie," as she was nicknamed, could really give you a good laugh!

One day, the famous American singer, Vickie Lynn, performed with the USO at the hospital and with the troupe was an Army Captain who was a damn good comedian. He could parle Francaise very well, so as Madame Shu-Shu and Gritty Gertie were present, he called Gertie to his side and asked her to say something in French. Gertie became so excited that all she could get out was "Oui, Oui, Oui, Oui." "Come on, Madame, parle Francaise," the Captain continued, but he got the same, "Oui, Oui, Oui, Oui." The Captain then gave up and everyone in the audience broke out laughing. Even Vickie Lynn stopped singing to join in the laughter. Gritty Gertie got more excited as she laughed with everyone else, and continued with, "Oui, Oui, Oui, Oui!" The comic Captain shook his head, then asked Gertie to join the USO troupe. "Oui,

Oui, Oui, Oui," was her reply, as she giggled and walked away, not knowing in the least what the Captain had said.

As the second week of my stay came to an end, I was much better and had even gained five pounds. My dizziness was on the wane, but the ears were still ringing off the hook. The strong medication I was taking every several hours eased my headaches which were vicious during the process of my recovery.

As the third week rolled around, Lieutenant Garcia and I were allowed to go out on pass from 1600 to 2300 hours. Our first outing took the two of us to the small Cafe Rouge in St. Denis, where we met several real young and pretty mademoiselles. We all had several glasses of vin rouge (red wine), then asked two of them to join us for a venture into Paris, which was only a metro ride away. After taking the metro (subway) into Paris proper, Garcia and I didn't drink any more vin rouge, as wine and medication don't mix. However, the mademoiselles drank some more with the fine bouillabaisse we all enjoyed in a nice cafe on the Champs-Elysees. After the meal at Cafe Rendevous, we all attended the opera, *Barber of Seville*, at the National Hall of Music (Paris Opera). By the time we arrived back in St. Denis it was 2300 hours, so after escorting the mademoiselles home, we stayed with them two more hours, as they were wonderful company. Arriving back at the hospital, we only received a short reprimand from our favorite nurse, who was waiting to treat us with some overdue medication.

For several more days, the Lieutenant and I stayed close, taking our medication and cooperating fully with the doctors and nurses. We were actually bucking to get out of this hospital and back on the line again, as the Third Army was moving ever closer in its fierce drive to the Rhine. My head pain was now becoming milder though the (ear) ringing never ceased, and I kept the latter to myself because in time it would gradually fade away, so I thought.

Toward the end of this third week, the Lieutenant and I managed to obtain a twenty-four-hour pass. Immediately we contacted Nicole and Jeannie who suggested we go to Compiegne, fifty miles north of Paris. Taking a fast train from Gare du Nord, out of St. Denis, we arrived in Compiegne in less than two hours. After checking in at the Hotel St. Jorge, we had chicken fricassee and vin blanc (white wine) in the dining room, then our own tour of sight-seeing. Nicole and Jeannie were from this city and really wanted to show us how proud they were of its splendor. They escorted us through one of the most fabulous museums that either of us had ever seen. There were some wonderful works of art on the walls and ceilings of this place of splendor. This vast stone structure was none other than Napoleon's Summer Palace. In the enclosed section of a vast courtyard were many beautifully well preserved carriages that transported the past rulers of France, going back in the centuries. We saw the carriages of the King Louis' from I to XIV, also Napoleon's and Josephine's and Marie Antoinette's. The German army was pushed out of Compiegne so fast that this palace of Napoleon's was hardly touched by war, as only a few of the "master's" art works were missing. With the day now at an end, the four of us went to a small cafe nearby where the wine and food were simple, but very enjoyable in the quiet atmosphere. Later, a young boy and girl came in, the boy with an accordion accompanied the girl's beautiful voice, in a very delightful musical entertainment. The music and vocal were captivating, but limited to old songs such as *La Paloma* and *La Golendrino*; however, they created a wonderful mood in this foursome that kept us dancing, singing along and enjoying the vin rouge until midnight in this quiet native French atmosphere.

In early morning, we checked out of the hotel, taking the fast electric train back to St. Denis, where we said farewell to Nicole and Jeannie, then checked back into the hospital right on time. After lunch at the cafeteria, where we had as Madame Shu-Shu would say, music (beans) and franks. Upon our return to the room, the Lieutenant and I were informed that our physicals would be taking place within the hour, and if all went well, we would be on our way back to the front in early morning. This was really music to our ears, because March was already here and General Patton's Third Army was moving ever closer to the formidable Rhine. Lieutenant Garcia and I wanted to get back to the outfit because once to the Rhine and across, General Patton would move the Third Army through Germany and Central Europe like crap going through a goose, as he would put it! We wanted to make sure that what was coming up would damn well include us!

Our physicals took place on time, and both of us were found fit to return to duty, but wouldn't be discharged from the hospital for another forty-eight hours, due to the outcome of certain tests.

The next day we were given twenty-four-hour passes to Paris and this turned out to be fabulous. Nicole and Jeannie were happy to be our sight-seeing guides in this city of fantasy when we broke the good news to them at the cafe in St. Denis First we visited the Arc de Triomphe, then Notre Dame, The Louvre, and its famous collection of art, and the Eiffel Tower. Along the West Bank of the Seine, we visited sidewalk cafes, then we crossed ancient bridges to do the same on the East Bank. After a visit and tour of Place Pigalle, we ended our tour at the "Folies Bergere," after which we boarded the metro and arrived back in St. Denis at midnight.

This was a real farewell party that Lieutenant Garcia and I arranged for our two mademoiselles. When we reached this little offbeat Cafe Rouge, the music was French and perfect for the four of us to dance by in this quiet little cafe, between sips of the finest Napoleon brandy. It was 0200 hours when the cafe closed, but after escorting Nicole and Jeannie to their apartment, the party continued, until daylight when we enjoyed crepe suzettes and cafe for the farewell breakfast.

Back to our hospital room at 0900 hours, we packed our gear, then were assigned to the barracks area. Our test reports were good, so Lieutenant Garcia and I would be leaving by truck in the evening hours on our journey back to the front. Sleeping on the assigned bunks from noon lunch until 1900 hours (along with about twelve other guys, including an infantry captain), we were loaded on a 6x6 truck, and off we sped toward the east, and on into the night.

Stopping in Reims, France, after midnight, we were treated to coffee and doughnuts by the Red Cross, then we hastened on into the dark night across the northern French countryside. This time we were joined with two trucks loaded with new replacements. Around nine in the morning; after a hell of a rough ride over still war ravaged roads, we arrived in a small suburb of Luxembourg City. Dismounting the trucks, we would be in this temporary replacement depot until reassignment, which would soon be forthcoming. Armed with some "C" rations, cigarettes, soap and chewing gum,

Lieutenant Garcia and I made up our minds to look up a family who had helped us during the hell of battle that once raged here. Darkness came while we were still trying to locate this family, but with a full moon rising to light our way the Lieutenant and I continued on. At the end of a moonlit street we came upon a girl we had met during the harsh winter here, her name was Clementine, and it so happened that she lived with the family we were seeking. In a few minutes, the three of us entered the shell and scrapnel ravaged apartment building where the Schmidt family occupied a second floor flat. When the door opened and Mama Schmidt saw who was there, she screamed with joy, "everybody come, is the Lieutenant Garcia and Buzz!" And did they ever come, the four girls, mama, papa, and two elderly ladies were all over us. After the initial greetings, we set all of our goodies on the long table, and mama Schmidt collected the "C" rations (meat and vegetable stew, Spam, canned fruit and chocolate bars) for preparation of the family's dinner meal. While mama and the two elderly ladies were preparing dinner, the daughters and papa entertained the Lieutenant and me with his accordion music, singing and dancing, along with some excellent cognac. As we were seated at the table, mama Schmidt brought that drab meat and vegetable stew in, wrapped in a golden crust, and the Spam had been dipped and fried in batter. She had also prepared and baked homemade brown bread which was served with the strawberry jam in the "C" ration and the hot Nescafe topped off this festive table, a meal fit for a king! This was a good catholic family, so everyone participated in grace, and by the time grace was finished, the Nescafe was getting cold. However, mama heated up the Nescafe again and this wonderful meal was soon consummed.

After a few hours of talking and enjoying the friendship of this poor family who befriended many of us infantrymen during the terrible winter of 1944-45, it was time to say farewell. Clementine walked with us back to the staging area, and as Lieutenant Garcia wasn't feeling too well, he decided to call it a night. Clementine and I continued to walk through the moonlit grotesque war ravaged streets to a small park where we found a place to sit, and talk until midnight. This was the last I saw of this wonderful girl, who was so sweet and understanding, a friend to all who knew her. When I walked her back home through the empty streets, the only things moving were the two of us and our shadows in the cold moonlight. "I will pray for your well being, to the end of this terrible war," Clementine said as we parted with a farewell kiss.

Back to the temporary quarters, I eased into my bunk next to Lieutenant Garcia, who was sounding off in his sleep like the whistle of a steam locomotive. At 0500 Lieutenant Garcia, four infantry replacements and I were called out. The sergeant who called us spoke up, "you may not like this assignment Lieutenant, you and your buddy, you are going to your same armored infantry battalion, but another Company as they are in bad need of a platoon and squad leader. Anyway it is orders, and I got to carry them out!" "No problem," said Lieutenant Garcia, "we are all in this damn war together, so let's get on the move, as long as we are still with the Third Army under "blood and guts," why the hell should we give a tinker's damn!" I could tell by the tone of his voice that Lieutenant Garcia was disappointed, and so was I, because my buddy, Hoffman, and I had been through hell together and this would end our close association in this war against the Nazis.

Our group was issued new M-1 rifles which were loaded with Cosmoline (preservative almost like glue) and after an hour's work with a small open coal fire, gasoline, and lots of rags to help us, we had those rifles gleaming. We were issued several banderillas of ammunition each, and with new helmets along with waterproof combat boots we were all set for the front. At breakfast, we had the traditional fried Spam, mashed dehydrated potatoes, and peas, with coffee so damn strong that it could easily walk.

After breakfast, new green combat jackets were issued along with new sleeping bags. The six of us were loaded on a weapons carrier, and traveling over bumpy, muddy shell pocked roads, we pulled into the German city of Trier on the Moselle, by nightfall. Trier was an ancient German city wrapped in history back even to the Roman times (Roman architectural ruins could still be observed, dating back to the age of Julius Caesar who was once there). The city hadn't changed much in two months, except that much rubble had been cleared from the roadway and streets to keep them passable. We all enjoyed a break provided by the Red Cross Canteen, coffee and doughnuts.

Then we were back on the road again in two hours, this time there were thirty-six of us in two trucks. Just before sundown our group stopped within a few miles of the Third Army front, which was closing in on the formidable Rhine near the great Rhineland city of Coblenz. Lieutenant Garcia and I had arrived just in time to take part in the historical crossing of the Rhine by the Third Army, under command of the most colorful General in the United States Army, George S. Patton, Jr. Wish us all the best of luck as we prepare to cross this mighty river.

Under cover of darkness, Lieutenant Garcia and I were picked up by a jeep with a thirty-caliber machine gun mounted on it. Using blackout lights, the driver took us through hostile territory on the edge of no man's land, to Company Headquarters in a log-reinforced dugout. There we received our front line assignments, and with the help of a Company runner, we took up our positions with the Platoon which was already dug in. Lieutenant Garcia filled in as Platoon leader, and not far away, I took up my position as squad leader. Neither of us had to dig in, as empty foxholes were readily available due to casualties from the eternal 88s!

Battleground, makeshift bunker, and last resting place of an enemy soldier, Germany 1945

Chapter 11
Across the Rhine, Central Europe and Victory

To be back on the front lines with the Third Army was great, even though Lieutenant Garcia and I were attached to another Company, we were where the need was critical. After a brilliant advance through the remaining eastern Rhineland, our spearhead of the Third Army reached the formidable Rhine at Oppenheim, Germany, south of Koblenz. It was a hell of a disappointment to find all the bridges demolished by a retreating Nazi army, but General Patton was letting nothing deter his Third Army's drive to victory.

The Rhine River was the last natural barrier to Germany's heartland, and even though bridges were destroyed, pontoon bridges were assembled by combat engineers, under sometimes intense fire. Under cover of darkness the division which our battalion was spearheading, moved out in an assault across the Rhine. We had now breached this natural barrier and set up a bridgehead on its eastern side. The date was now March 23, 1945, and the way everything was going in our favor, the Nazis could not hold out for very long.

Lieutenant Garcia was now Acting Company Commander and a damn good one at that. My squad were nearly all new replacements, but they turned out to be excellent combat soldiers, and knew how to carry out orders given them. The tank battalion we spearheaded with was tough, as the M-26 Pershing tanks could blast the hell out of the Nazi Panther and Tiger tanks with the 90 mm guns they carried. Then, also, our tanks could outrun and out-maneuver the larger Tiger tanks of up to 72 tons.

Sometimes I wondered how my buddy, Hoffman, was doing and I imagined he was thinking the same about me. But no news, so the saying goes, is good news, and maybe in the future we would meet again. I was now teamed up with a damn good infantryman, who was an expert in all weapons that we used, especially the rocket launching bazooka. Kramer was from Brooklyn, and was as tough as they come; also, he like myself, had a dire determination to get this war over as quickly as possible! "Buzz," he said one day, "I have more than one reason to be in the front lines. Besides my patriotic duty to my country, I have some close kin who were victims of the Holocaust, and hope to help liberate any who may be alive!" "I can understand that," Kramer, I answered, "as you fight with much vengeance, but yet you are humane and fair with the enemy. Even though you speak the Deutsch fluently and question prisoners we capture, abstracting much valuable information, I have never seen you mistreat any of them. To sum it all up, Kramer, you are a damn good soldier and I am lucky to have you in this squad!"

On March 24th, General Patton's bridgehead at Oppenheim was approximately eight miles wide and our Third Army tanks along with armored infantry were about ten miles to the east, heading toward Frankfurt on Main. The advance to Frankfurt was definitely not a piece of cake. One such time, when our platoon was pinned down by a barrage of 88 mm artillery, we were ordered to dig in. Fortunately, most of us found shallow trenches left by the retreating enemy. Taking cover next to Kramer and me were a very comical pair called "Junior" and "Heavy." Heavy was a large ex-paratrooper who was tough as nails, and Junior was just a young inexperienced replacement. This day Junior pulled out his pocket Bible and began reading it silently, while Heavy was laughing at him. All at once a volley of screaming meemies whistled in and began exploding all around. Momentarily it was quiet, except for Heavy who bellowed out, "Junior, when you finish reading that Bible, pass it over here!" Later on that evening, P-47 fighter bombers came over and dive-bombed the hell out of the enemy gun and tank positions. Before dusk we moved out of our holding position and went on the offensive again.

There was much mopping up to do before we reached a fairly large German village, which fell into our hands without much resistance. While flushing out some leftover snipers, (hard core SS), Kramer and I came upon an Army Chaplain, so we spoke, and I noticed he was packing a 45, holstered on his pistol belt. "Father," I said, "what's with the 45? I didn't think Chaplains carried arms!" "Well, son," the Chaplain answered, "you should know that the Good Lord helps those who help themselves." When the mopping up was finished, we moved to the eastern outskirts, where the decision was made to hold until first light.

There was a farmhouse on the northern edge of this village that hadn't been checked out, so Kramer and I volunteered to this assignment. When we reached this farmhouse with weapons drawn, the door opened and a little old housefrau stood alone lamenting, "der Deutschland ist kaput!" (Meaning Germany is finished.) Then two young frauleins came up behind her begging in broken but understandable English, "Please Amerikans, do not harm us!" Kramer assured them in German that definitely no harm would come to them. After searching the house, as was necessary, these people treated us like family. They were poor, but they shared with us some fine cognac, apple strudel and coffee, which really hit the spot. The three of them gave us a kiss on the cheek as we departed for our holding perimeter. The youngest, a pretty blonde whispered in my ear, "Amerikan, you come back see me tonight!" I didn't take her up on that because during those times you could be the bait for a trap!

The following morning at first light, the Pershings revved up and on to the east we headed with the great city of Frankfurt on the Main River, our initial goal. Passing through a German town close onto Frankfurt, even after the Burghmaster (Mayor) just about gave us the key to the city, an elderly frau fired a Panzerfaust (German bazooka) at one of our new Pershing tanks, damaging its track.

The Third Army ran into some resistance in the Rhine - Main areas, but nothing that we couldn't take care of. We could see, especially after Frankfurt and Hanau fell, that the end was near for the Third Reich. The cities of Frankfurt, Hanau, and Offenbach were racked by destruction, with piles of rubble in just about every street. In these cities, we encountered some street, and house-to-house fighting, but as our armored infantry moved with the spearheading tanks, the regular infantry was left with most of the dirty mopping up operations. I have a great respect for them as they do a wonderful job in combat.

Upon leaving the great Frankfurt area in ruins, we advanced across the German countryside, taking towns and villages as we reached them. There was no stopping the Third Army which had already taken nearly a half million prisoners since Avranches, France. This was considerably more than any other Army had taken during the liberation of Europe.

On the Third Army's drive across Germany, it reached the point where resistance was so damn sporadic, that our armored infantry could ride the tanks and half-track sometimes for hours before dismounting to knock out opposition. There were displaced persons and German citizens with their scant belongings taking to the highways and byways, many in the path of our advance. It was a very sad time, as these people had nothing. This was the plight of thousands of homeless people whose lives had been changed forever by this war.

Overrunning and liberating the Buchenwald and Ohrdruf concentration camps were shocking sights for anyone to see how inhumane the Nazis' could treat another race of people. Real death camps such as these were grim reminders of how human beings had been starved to skin and bones, beaten, and many had been put to death. Many were machine-gunned and their bodies were dumped in mass graves, one such was left uncovered, due to the fast advance of the Third Army, and the Nazis quick withdrawals. Anyway, one would have to see the aftermath of these Nazi atrocities to actually believe that civilized people could be so inhumane to any race. Believe me, this really happened, and every American soldier who saw it was appalled. Those who were responsible for the Holocaust will surely have an appointment in hell, if it exists!

Many of the Germans' homes in the populated areas that we passed through, were vacated temporarily. At times, when a house was checked out, there would be a small sign, "Please do not harm our little home." We didn't, but if one needed to use the bathroom you had better check for wires leading to boobytraps.

Upon reaching the great historical city of Nuremberg, we found it almost totally destroyed and the people were living in what was left of gutted buildings and cellars under the rubble. The whole countryside was beautiful, but dotted in ruins, both old and new!

On April 13, 1945, we received the news of the death of our Commander-in-Chief, President Franklin D. Roosevelt. This was a very sad day for all American forces, and all Americans, along with the Allied nations. This man was a real prince, and a great humanitarian. I could remember the hunger pangs that my family and I had experienced during the Great Depression. Also, it came to mind how my father, mother, and brother had been given temporary jobs with the WPA, which helped put food on the table during these times.

We heard the news from "Axis Sally" from time to time over our tank's radio and she carried on a rumor that the "elite troopen" would make a last fanatical stand somewhere near the Austrian border. "Yanks," she boasted, "you are going to be annihilated when and where you least expect it." "Bull," said Kramer to some of the replacements who almost believed her. "The Heinies have shot their big gun, and everything you hear from Sally is bull, as she is scared out of her pants, like all of the damn Nazis." "Kramer is right, guys," I put in, "pay no attention to that Nazi bitch!"

The end of the Third Reich was now in sight, as our spearhead now attached to the Third Army's Fifth Corps, crossed the German-Czechoslovakian border, then on to Pilsen. Pilsen, the home of the Skoda Works and Pilsner Beer was entered very easily. The Czech people, especially the young ladies were overly happy to welcome their liberation, and we really had a night on the town with these happy people and the Pilsner Beer!

We were now in May of 1945, and the Russians had already taken Vienna. Our infantry, along with the tank battalion we were attached to, received orders to head south, with another armored force we would meet along the German-Austrian border near Passau, the southern shoulder of the Third Army would then sweep down the Danube to meet another victorious army along its north bank. Our two victorious Allied armies met at Linz, Austria, where Americans and Russians enjoyed friendship, toasted with super strong vodka in Hitler's own hometown!

Another death camp was liberated close-by Linz also, Mauthausen, which was even worse than Buchenwald. How in hell can man be so inhumane and cruel, I shall never know! This was a time that every American will always remember, especially those of us who had spent over two years in the European Theatre of operations. Germany surrendered unconditionally on May 8th and one minute past midnight May 9, 1945, it took effect.

Chapter 12
Postwar Cry of the Werewolf

The time was 0001 (one minute past midnight), May 9, 1945, when the unconditional surrender of all Nazi forces took place at Rheims, France. Now all Europeans were free of the Nazi tidal wave which had engulfed them for so long a time. Thousands of more prisoners were taken, along the north bank of the Danube, which would bring the Third Army's total to nearly a million, since Normandy. The meeting of two victorious armies (Russian and American) touched off a great series of celebrations. The Russians furnished the vodka, the Austrians the beer, and Americans the food. What a wonderful time it was in Linz, Austria. Some of the prettiest frauleins in Europe lived in Linz and music, dance, strong Austrian beer, and Russian vodka were prevalent, especially during the off-duty hours. As the great celebration of the victory in Europe slowed after a few fantastic days and nights in Linz, my Company was ordered to the Frankfurt-Hanau area.

A group of hard-line fanatic Nazi SS became active on a small scale. Sniper fire, although sporadic was reported, especially around the outskirts of these war-ravaged cities where American officers were living temporarily in German residences. This fanatical group was known as the "werewolves," and, like the mythical werewolf, they were mostly active at night.

Our armored infantry company with First Lieutenant Garcia as Acting Commander, pulled out of Linz, Austria, early one morning. This was a perfect day, with blue skies and bright sunshine, as the M-26 tanks and half-tracks roared westward along the north bank of the Danube toward the German border. Passing through quaint Austrian villages along the way, we received many waves and greetings as we stopped at times for breaks. Many of the Austrians showered us with handshakes and kisses, also these villagers brought out refreshments. In one small village close to the German border the villagers came out with accordion music, pretty frauleins, and beer, so we had a short street dance.

Crossing the German border at noon, we wasted no time in crossing the German countryside, as by dusk, our unit pulled into the outskirts of Nuremberg, Germany. After setting up a bivouac, the field kitchen went into action, serving a fine meal of steak, dehydrated potatoes and peas. The bread was freshly baked and the coffee was real, a damn good dinner it was for this war weary, tired group of infantrymen and tankers.

After we were fed, the leftovers were given to displaced persons, both German and other Europeans who waited patiently on the edge of our bivouac. Those people I really felt sorry for, as they had absolutely nothing, no homes or jobs, just wandering from place to place, expressionless. The war had changed their lives forever. Lieutenant Garcia and I were discussing the plight of these displaced persons, and he said to me, "Buzz, you and I may not realize it at present, but the damn war had, and will, take a hell of a toll on our lives. They will never in this world be the same again!" "You are right, Garcia," I replied, "the hell of war is not easily put aside. Even now we have to flush out a damn bunch of snipers."

Just as I shed my combat jacket and shoes, getting ready to get in my sleeping bag, a slight figure came up beside me with a blanket. I could see by the pale moonlight, that it was a very petite girl with a boyish haircut. Then she spoke in broken English, "American, may I stay here beside you? A mans zat is among displaced peoples is bother me, so you look nice and maybe you be kind and give to me protection from him? I am displaced peoples from Polish Ukraine, and mine name, Natasha.""Yes, Natasha," I answered, "you may stay right here at my side, and you will be protected from harm." The girl then spread out her blanket and stretched out on it. We talked for a little while, then she was asleep. Kramer, who was in his sleeping bag on the other side of mine, whispered, "Buzz, remember, no sleepwalking tonight!" "Mind your own damn business, Kramer," I whispered back, as I dropped off in a fitful sleep. I did not sleep well, due to spending so much time in combat, I was in the habit of sleeping very light, just about anything would awaken and put me immediately on the alert. Before first light, I awakened with a start as I detected a man's creeping figure moving close to Natasha's sleeping figure. Taking the 45 from the holster, I waited until the figure leaned over to check the blanket. At that moment, I raised up in the sleeping bag and stuck the pistol barrel in his ribs. When this happened, that sob took off so damn fast, that he almost ran smack into one of the roving guards who took him into custody immediately. Natasha was so very grateful to find someone who cared and gave her the will to live, and someday find her family, who had been sent to a death camp by the Nazis.

With the help of Kramer and "Sonny," I was able to disguise Natasha and take her with us the following day to Frankfurt. Natasha, at a displaced persons camp outside the city near our bivouac, found an older sister for whom she had been wishing to locate since Nuremberg fell. The way the sisters found each other was purely by accident. The sister came to the bivouac area with other displaced humanity for leftovers, and Natasha, standing behind me, recognized her, then I called the sister over. They must have embraced each other for at least five minutes, then Natasha embraced me and with an unforgettable farewell kiss, said, "my soldier, may the 'Blessing of the Virgin be ever with you!'"

As the two happy sisters departed for the camp, Lieutenant Garcia who was close-by, said to one of the squad leaders, "Tommy, didn't I just see Buzz kiss a boy?" "Hell no," said Tommy, "she warn't no boy, not with doze twin 38s under that thare shirt she had on!" With that Lieutenant Garcia winked at me and went on about his duties, without asking any more questions.

With the field kitchen beef stew dinner over, and all leftovers given to the displaced persons, the cooks who secured the mess tent for the night, hit the sack. I was called from my sleeping bag at midnight, as was my whole platoon. The moon was full in a cloudless sky as we relieved our buddies, and began walking the perimeter with our loaded, shouldered M-1 rifles. All went well and it would have been a beautiful night, except for the war ruins which were visible all around with such a bright moon. Kramer and I passed close to a once beautiful church, now in ruins, in our rounds. As we inspected these ruins, like a miracle, the only thing left standing inside was a perfect statue of the Blessed Virgin Mary!

Later, around 0200 in the early morning, sniper fire at intervals began to hamper us to the point that when we heard a crack, both would take cover in any low place. In a few minutes, Lieutenant Garcia joined Kramer and me with more men from the Company. As we advanced in a staggered formation toward a ruined building a few more shots were fired, and there were several bloodcurdling howls, then all was quiet. On our way back, I asked Lieutenant Garcia, "of all the infantry outfits in Europe, some have only been here a short time, why in hell do they have to pick a unit that has been through the whole war to do this job?" With a big laugh, Lieutenant Garcia answered, "Buzz, as I told you long ago, be damned if I know how the upper crust thinks! Maybe it is because we are darn good!" I think everybody in the outfit felt the same in this situation. The war was now officially over, and the Nazis had surrendered unconditionally, but this unit was still in a postwar police action with a bunch of sniping fanatics. Regardless of the dangers we faced in this operation, we would give it our best, and clear the area of these so-called "werewolves."

After a few hours of sleep, our platoon moved quietly through the ruins into a wooded area, where we captured two young Nazis who had been a part of the Hitler Jungend, asleep in foxholes, with their mausers loaded.

Back to our bivouac area we turned the youths over to the Military Police. Then my platoon moved out to another area close to Hanau, where we were assigned to pull guard duty, around a group of German homes. These homes had escaped the ravages of war, and were now being used to house some pencil pushing Army officers. All but one of these homes housed the officers, and that one belonged to a pretty German doctor, who owned it. Everyone in this group of homes had been harassed by the "werewolves," and a few had been hit. Our job was to patrol this whole perimeter twenty-four hours a day, using deadly force, if necessary, to break up the terrorizing werewolves! I was assigned to the street which included the doctor's home. She lived alone and was very friendly, especially with me, as my orders put me in charge of the key to let her in and out. Sometimes, I would engage in conversations with her, even though the "no fraternization law" was in effect. She would leave early in the mornings and return in late evenings, after treating patients all day. She was a real humanitarian, treating displaced persons as well as German citizens with very scant medical supplies.

As far as action was concerned, we had enough of it, but were fortunate enough to have only a few casualties thus far. The fire from the "werewolves" was very sporadic, and our units were able to flush them out of their makeshift bunkers. However, more youths would take their places, and start up all over again with sporadic fire and "wolf howls!"

During the daylight hours, things were usually quiet, but at night, especially moonlit nights, sniper fire would begin and continue until after dawn. Most of the time it was sporadic, but that was too damn much, also, these damn Nazi "werewolves" sounded off with howls like nature's own wolves in the wild. It was really uncanny!

These so-called "werewolves" had been also terrorizing a slave labor camp in another location nearby, where Russian, Polish, and other nationalities were imprisoned by the Nazis. These unfortunate people had been harassed by the German citizens, besides being forced into slave labor by the Nazi regime, and now were receiving more punishment from these die-hards. Even though these displaced persons were being processed by a special committee, it could be months before they could begin on their lives again and some never would! They sure in hell didn't need these damn terrorists to further their depression, so my platoon was damn well going to do something about it. Under command of Lieutenant Garcia, we made a clean sweep of the whole area around this infamous camp, staying for about a week, flushing out a dozen or more of these groups of Nazi youth, which were turned over to the Military Police. There were no fatalities, but several causalities occurred on both sides. These "werewolves" were more like rats than anything else, when cornered, just a bunch of brain-washed Nazi Jugend (Nazi Youth Movement). Once back in their homes, with proper raising, they probably would someday become good German citizens.

Some of the displaced persons in the former slave labor camp wanted to be freed before processing, but my outfit had experienced the results of that situation in the recent past. During the last month of combat, we liberated one such camp consisting of Polish and Russian displaced persons, letting them go free. Be damned if my Company didn't have to go back and round them up again. Many times in their years of confinement, German citizens had taunted them unmercifully, as they passed the camp, even on their Sunday walks. When they were freed, all of their pent–up hatred for the citizens of the nearby town sent them on a crusade for vengeance. When the displaced persons reached this town they burst into homes and began throwing furniture, along with other items out of windows, and if the Germans got in their way, they were also thrown out. When my Company received the message for help, we went back a few miles, reasoned with their leaders, and put a stop to the rampaging. As they were being calmed down, they were temporarily restrained back in the camp until they could be processed. In the meantime they received food rations and Military Police set up a guard unit. When that situation was under control, my Company caught up with our battalion and tanks, spearheading the Third Army, and continued on our vast drive to victory!

Getting back to our assignment in the residential area outside of Hanau, my platoon took up where they left off. Once we had relieved those who had replaced us for the mission, we just settled down in our old routine, guarding the residences, while also flushing out the troublemakers, or what was left of them! The young female doctor was glad to see me back again, and sometimes during my off-duty hours, I would join her for tea, and also at times, a glass of vintage Moselle, which was a rarity. She was a fine lady, and could carry on any conversation in almost perfect English. She was definitely not a Nazi!

Everything began to change rapidly in the month of June. Lieutenant Garcia became Captain Garcia, Company Commander, and I took his place as Acting Platoon Leader. Both he and I, as well as Kramer, had more than enough points to get out of the army, but continued on this assignment until just about all the danger had passed, and thus the Army of Occupation took over where we left off.

In July, Garcia, Kramer and I received orders for zone of the interior and what a happy day that was, to be returning to the United States after twenty-eight months. The three of us packed our gear early one morning in July 1945, and a jeep picked us up at Company Headquarters for a ride to the makeshift airport outside the ruins of Frankfurt.

Chapter 13
To Valenciennes

Arriving at the temporary airport near Frankfurt, the three of us waited until noon before our flight departed. Strapped in our bucket seats, along with about thirty Air Force personnel in a well used C-47, we finally took off at 1700 hours for Valenciennes, France. During takeoff the runway was so short that the landing gear knocked down part of a fence as it struggled to clear some trees ahead. I am quite sure the cargo carried by this C-47 was the culprit in getting airborne.

This was a very pretty day as the pilot passed low over Paris so we could get a bird's-eye view of this fabulous city through the portholes over our seats. Passing low over the Champs-Elysees, everyone had a good view of the Arc de Triomphe, Notre Dame, the Seine with its fabulous bridges, and the Eiffel Tower. When we arrived in the beautiful city of Valenciennes, France, all of us were transported to a barracks in an Air Force facility, where we would stay until further orders were forthcoming.

After being processed, Captain Garcia, Kramer, and I went out on the town. The three of us departed the barracks at dusk, and walked all the way into the heart of the city, with our way lighted by a fantastic full moon. As we walked along the way, I made the remark, "guys, I don't remember a time when I felt any better than this. It is like walking the stairway to the stars, no 88s nor screaming meemies to worry about. Peace comes with a price, but it was damn well worth it!" "Agreed, Buzz," Captain Garcia spoke up, "and no damn buzz bombs passing over our heads sounding like a farm tractor, and never knowing when it is going to cut off, fall out of the sky and explode like a volcano." "Youse guys," put in Kramer, "cut out the damn bull, the damn war is over and right now we got it made, savvy?" We all then had a big laugh, and the first cafe that came into view was our destination. Then we looked around, and there it was staring us right in the face, Cafe de Oro (Cafe of Gold), so we proceeded in and right into the company of three of the most beautiful mademoiselles in all of France. They gave out their "bon jours" with ardent smiles attached and right away this trio took the bait! Not one of these mademoiselles could speak a word of English, but they could laugh, drink vin rouge and dance to their native music. So we talked with them in the limited French (picked up during our past associations) and danced the night away. The Cafe closed at midnight, so as we departed with the mademoiselles, they insisted that we go to their maison (home).

As we walked down the street, all was dark except for the full moon. The girl with me pointed up into the sky and whispered, "la luna" (the moon), so I whispered back "oui, mademoiselle, la luna, bon!" These girls were all sisters, but we didn't know this was the situation until we reached their apartment. It was a well-furnished and attractive place, also they had a nice radio and record player, which were put to good use as we danced the early morning hours away. Annette and Marie worked as secretaries, while the youngest, Cecile, went to a small college nearby. She was my date, and by a slight margin, was the prettiest and the best dancer. These girls had a rough time during the Nazi occupation, so the three of us were damn well going to show them a wonderful time while here in their fair city.

The party broke up around 0300 hours, with a promise that we would meet them at the same time, same place, the following night. With a good morning kiss, the trio of us headed into what we thought was the right direction. How wrong we were, as sometimes these foreign cities can fool you. Finally, we found ourselves in a part of this city that would damn nearly compare with New York's Bowery.

Valenciennes was a beautiful French city, situated in northern France near its border with Belgium. Every city I had ever visited up until that time has slums (whether in Europe or the United States of America), Captain Garcia, Kramer and I found ourselves totally lost in this rough "off limits" area, at the critical hour of 0500 in the early morning. As we turned around to retrace our tracks, five tough-looking characters blocked our way, coming at us from a dark alley. The only thing we could do was fight our way out of this human blockade. By forming a triangle, swinging and bashing these tough-looking thieves, we were able to deck all of them; however, more of these characters were coming from behind to gang up on us. Knowing that we couldn't take on all of them, Kramer immediately went for his small Italian revolver from which he fired a couple of rounds over the heads of them and they vanished into the holes from whence they came. Retracing our tracks once more down a narrow street, a woman emptied a chamber pot from a fourth floor window and that damn stuff barely missed us.. "Let's get the hell out of here fast," Garcia said, as we broke into a run.

This trio finally got back to the barracks in time for morning roll call, and afterwards, hit the sack. Since we had no duties to perform, this trio spent all day in the sack. Dinner chow was served in the main mess hall at 1700 hours (5:00 p.m.), so after a fine meal, we shaved, showered, dressed, and with signed passes, went out to meet our dates again at Cafe de Oro. Our friends were a little late, so we had several shots of prima cognac while waiting for them. My Zippo lighter was out of fluid, so I ordered a double shot of Calvados (not unlike white lightning), filled the lighters of Garcia and mine, then Kramer drank the rest.

The mademoiselles were an hour late, but they showed up at the time the local music began and Cafe de Oro came alive. The music was vintage as well as the red wine, so we danced to this haunting music, sipped the wine, laughed and partied the night away. Back to the apartment under the light of the full moon again, we danced to music from Radio Paris. The night was so beautiful with a moon so full and bright that we all decided to go out and enjoy this beauty of Mother Nature. The mademoiselles suggested a park which was not far away, so each couple split up after reaching this fantastic place. Cecile and I found a deserted concrete park bench where we took our places with la luna directly overhead. It was an unforgettable summer night. La luna's pale light filtered through the fully leafed trees of this unique park, casting shadows over the green terrain. There was only one thing wrong in this otherwise perfect setting, and that was a premonition of fate that was coming over me. I had experienced this sensation before and as it had always turned out positive, I became instantly alert sensing a danger approaching. Looking around, I noticed that one of the shadows created by the light of la luna was moving. I whispered to Cecile, putting my hand over her mouth to be very quiet, and she understood. Just as a dark cloud covered the moon, I slipped to the ground and crawled to a clump of bushes, then waited in the path of this intruder. As the shadow eased by, close to my hiding place, I reached out, took hold of it's legs and this phantom of the night fell like a boulder. Instantly, I was on his back with a bear hold, pinning him to the ground, then with my right arm I hit his hand hard enough to make him drop the knife he was wielding, and Cecile grabbed it. Then I grabbed him by the neck and belt, standing him up straight. The way things turned out was different than what I had expected. The would-be assailant was a poor, ragged vagabond who really looked the part. All he could speak was sign language, and it was obvious that he was a half-starved deaf mute. Making signs that he and his family were hungry and desperate, softened my feelings quite a lot. So much that I handed him a 500 franc note, and sent him on his way, minus the knife. After all the war left a mark on all who had experienced and lived through it.

With that episode over, Cecile and I went back to the park bench and enjoyed much more of nature's beauty, before joining the other two couples, and heading back to the apartment. On the way back, we purchased a bottle of vin rouge from a wine shop and at the apartment, sipped wine and listened to excellent music from the BBC.

Leaving the apartment at 0500 hours in early morning, the three of us made sure that we stayed on the right track back to the barracks. On the way I made the remark, "guys, I wonder how long we will be here in the city of Valenciennes before returning to the United States?" Captain Garcia replied, "very frankly, Buzz, after meeting Annette, I really don't give a damn." "Same here," said Kramer, "after meeting the likes of Marie." "OK, guys," I concluded, "count me in with Cecile!"

Arriving back at the barracks, this trio slept for half a day, then with passes, until the following morning at 0800 hours, the time expanse belonged to us. The day was perfect weather-wise, so we must have walked at least twenty miles, marveling at the architectural beauty of Valenciennes. The museums, cathedrals and many other places of interest were breathtaking. France was a beautiful country, but more so in peace than in war.

Meeting the mademoiselles again, for dinner at the Cafe de la Peuple (Cafe of the People), where the food proved to be superior to any other cafe, brought happy smiles to their pretty faces. Later, all of us ventured back to our old standby, Cafe de Oro, where we sipped the vin rouge and again danced the night away to the old French music played beautifully by accordian and guitar. Back to the apartment of the mademoiselles, walking under la luna's full phase, bright as daylight, it was like walking through a romantic fairy tale. At that time Cecile told me in some of the broken English she had picked up from our group, "Buzz, you no go back to America, you stay Valenciennes, marry with Cecile?" This girl was very serious. When we reached our destination, I would talk with Garcia as it seemed that we were all in the same boat. These girls wanted American husbands! Calling Garcia aside, I put all the cards on the table as I spoke out, "Garcia, I damn well think we are going overboard with these French sisters, because Cecile already is talking marriage!" "So is Annette," Garcia answered, "but what the hell, just remember, these pretty mademoiselles are enjoying the nice things our money can buy them, as much as we are enjoying their company." "OK, buddy," I replied, "when we look at the situation that way, you are absolutely right!" That situation was conclusive now as far as I was concerned, as I walked over, took Cecile in my arms, and we began to tango to the beautiful Spanish music from Radio Madrid.

Our trio departed the apartment in time to walk to the base and turn in our passes just at 0800, expiration time. This was a special day, payday, so our alarm was set, as we damn well wouldn't miss the paymaster! Kramer and I reached the pay line about the same time, Captain Garcia was a little late, but was putting his shoes on when we left the room, so joined us shortly. Garcia and Kramer received their full pay, but due to the destruction of the half-track that my records were on during the Bulge, I could only receive partial pay. Anyway, if one of this close knit trio had money, we all did! We were comrades in war, and also in peace. In other words, the three of us were the kind of friends that no amount of money could make a difference. We were friends for life!

Before the three of us picked up our passes this day, we had orders to report to headquarters and meet with the transportation officer. The Army Air Corps Captain was awaiting our arrival, so right away he gave us travel orders. "Captain Garcia, you and your men were due out of here a week ago, but somehow your travel orders were sidetracked. Anyway, tomorrow at 1200 hours (noon), you three will fly out of this base to the Cherbourg, France, area. There you will be processed, then board the SS *Mariposa* for your return to the United States. I really don't understand why they sent you to this base in the first place, unless they were overloaded in the debarkation areas." Then I asked, "are we free to pick up our passes and go into Valenciennes tonight, Captain?" "Yes, definitely," he replied, "your passes will be good until 0800 in the morning, so have a ball!" "We will," I replied, as the three of us headed for the main gate where our passes were all signed and ready.

"Garcia," I asked, "how are we going to handle this with the present 'loves of our lives'?" Garcia's answer to this was "Buzz, we will just tell it as it is. They know damn well that we are soldiers, and, therefore, have to follow orders!"

The French sisters were on time when this trio arrived at Cafe de Oro. After a bottle of vin rouge was consumed, all of us went to the Cafe de la Peuple where a fine meal of bouillabaisse was enjoyed. Afterward, we walked through the park, where I made the decision to break the news to Cecile, about my latest orders. Garcia and Kramer also had come to that same decision, I found out later that night. "Cecile," I whispered, as we were seated by the little swan lake, "I do not like this, but du'mar parte America (tomorrow I leave for America). "Oh, no, no parte Cecile, you stay!" "I cannot stay, because I am soldier in my country's Army," I replied in a nice way. She understood, as she said, "Cecile comprehend," and with that came a wonderful smile and kiss in the moonlit surroundings. I know that she was sad, but so was I, at this time, and we both made the best of the situation. Captain Garcia and Kramer had also given out the disappointing news to Annette and Maria and I think all were taking it as well as could be expected.

On the way back to the apartment, we stopped at a little shop where wine, cognac and snacks were purchased for our farewell party, as we wined, dined and danced to delightful music until dawn broke over the horizon. Parting was really beautiful sorrow, as three soldiers kissed their pretty French mademoiselles au revoir and faded into the twilight.

Chapter 14
Back to the Good Old United States of America

Upon returning to the Air Force barracks by sunrise, this trio packed our bags, then were able to get a few hours sleep before call out for our noon flight to Cherbourg, France. Flying out on a B-26 was no picnic, as the three of us rode in the waist and tail sections, taking up the empty spaces that gunners occupied during combat. Landing at the makeshift airfield in Cherbourg was rough as the plane damn nearly overshot the runway. Anyway we arrived at our destination safely, and were whisked away to one of the processing centers by jeep. It was either Camp Lucky Strike or Camp Philip Morris, anyway it was the camp nearest the port of Cherbourg.

The SS *Mariposa* had not yet made arrival, so this trio would have nearly a week to wait. After all the paper work was finished, the three musketeers had a nice dinner and with a few thousand francs each, we hit the town! "Garcia," I said, "It sure in hell is not like it was when we made the drive across France during the liberation. Everything was free then, and now we have to pay through the nose!" "Damn right, Buzz, that's the appreciation we get, but hell, they got to make a living too," he laughed. "Come on youse guys let's find a cafe with some good time mademoiselles to lash on to while the night is still young," yelled out Kramer! And that is exactly what we did. On a side street off the main drag in Cherbourg, there was a cabaret all lit up and really jumping with music. There were beaucoup mademoiselles and the music was fantastic. A band was playing such songs as "You Belong to My Heart, Piano Concerto in B Flat Minor," and "Chopin's Polonaise" or "Til the End of Time." This was enough to drive these three infantrymen and probably a hundred more combat veterans crazy as hell. "Some night, this is going to be," said Garcia as we entered this "Cabaret Europa."

No sooner than when we reached the crowded bar, three of the prettiest mademoiselles around lashed onto this trio. Finding a table in this overloaded cabaret was one hell of a job, but we finally found one in a corner where the band was close-by. This entire cabaret was a dance floor, so after the three couples had consumed a liter of strong cognac, all began dancing to the new American hit, "Sentimental Journey." After several more dances, we decided to take a break, as the band finished the beautiful "Til the End of Time" from "Chopin's Polonaise."

With the second liter of the strong liquor, Calvados, being rapidly consumed, we were all beginning to feel our oats. However, the six of us were minding our own business, but in a crowd like this, there is always a troublemaker. A big loud mouthed Corporal from the Supply Service came by our table, stopped and made an insulting remark to Garcia. The character yelled out, "what the hell is a damn half-breed doing with double railroad tracks on his collar?" Well, I knew then that all of hell was going to take place, as Garcia was half-Mexican and half-Apache Indian, very proud of his heritage, and when Captain Garcia stood up showing a slight figure about five feet, eight inches, this big Corporal took a swing at him. Garcia ducked, then swinging with all his might, knocked the smart ass over two tables. Then hell did break loose, as a "free-for-all" developed, and as it progressed, it was every soldier for himself. After the three of us took on and knocked down at least two each, we actually fought our way to the exit where our mademoiselles were waiting. "Come with us Americans, we take you home, be safe for everyones, after clean up, you stay," Andrea, the mademoiselle I was with demanded in no uncertain terms. That is exactly what we did, and it was best for all. On the way, stopping by a small shop, I bought a long loaf of French bread, cheese and three liters of red wine to tide us over until the next day.

These ladies had a nice flat with a radio (music from Paris and Madrid) we danced until the early hours, enjoying intermissions with wine and snacks. As it was Saturday night when we arrived at the mademoiselles' flat and did not leave until Sunday evening, we all enjoyed a nice dinner of bouillabaisse at Cafe Normandie. Back to another cabaret Sunday night, it was altogether different, no fights, just wine sipping and dancing until closing.

Back to camp around 0600 Monday morning, we slept until noon, at which time lunch was served in the mess hall and afterward, our group was put on alert to move out. I am quite sure that every soldier who boarded the SS *Mariposa* (10,000 plus) had a complete set of service records, except me. My records, destroyed in combat still had not been straightened out, but I was now getting ready to board the ship that would sail in thirty-six hours for the good old United States with Boston, Massachusetts, as destination. My records would be replaced, at best in Camp Devers, Massachusetts.

The ship, moored in Cherbourg, began loading troops Monday night, continued through Tuesday and sailed for Boston Wednesday at 0800 hours. The weather was nice all the way across the North Atlantic, so we made arrival at 0800 hours the following Tuesday.

The ship was moored by 1000 hours, and when we debarked, everyone was given a banana and a half pint of fresh milk before boarding a train for Camp Devers. When the train arrived at our destination, the three of us were assigned to the same barracks, only Captain Garcia was downstairs, and Kramer and I were upstairs.

Anyway, we all got together the first night and went out on the town of Falmouth. That outing turned out to be a big mistake, because meeting up with a few of the guys from the Airborne Division that we helped to relieve during the Battle of Bastogne, everyone participated in another celebration of victory. There were no fights but the happy noisy get together of combat soldiers was too much for the bartender, so he called the MPs. When they arrived, with swinging clubs (which was totally unnecessary) several of us were hit, we damn well confiscated their clubs and after that everything simmered down. The clubs were returned by Captain Garcia who rode to the MP Station where he called a Colonel, who gave the MP Commander hell, and had them take us back to the barracks. No charges were due nor were any filed, but from then on we were very careful to choose the places to frequent.

One day Kramer and I were walking through the upper floor of the barracks to the outside stairway, when someone yelled out "Halt!" We looked around and there was a Private, drunk as he could be pointing a 45 at us. Several guys were standing around this character, scared to move, so I put my arms in the air, walked up to him as if I had given up, then quickly let my left arm come down and knocked the 45 right out of his hand. When it hit the floor, Kramer picked it up, so I said to this character, "you stupid sob, you are damn lucky this time, but next time you won't be."

Kramer and I then went on our way with the 45 that wouldn't be in that guy's hand again.

For the next week, all three of us stayed close to Camp, only at night did we go out to the clubs on base, and beer parties at one of the post exchanges. Keeping a low profile, we three stayed out of trouble and enjoyed a good time. There were always dances at one of the officers' and enlisted men's clubs and girls were brought in by bus from schools and colleges close-by, never a dull moment.

One morning I was called to the records office where I reported to the First Lieutenant in charge. I knocked, walked in, saluted, after which my salute was returned and he waved me over to his desk. "Have a seat and I'll be right with you," the Lieutenant said. "We have temporary records on you but I need some more information to go on these records in order to make them permanent." "Understood," I replied, "but we better have Captain Garcia present to verify, after all he and I have been together for over a year." "Right," he agreed, as the Captain was sent for and reported to the office within minutes. As the questions were asked about my duty, both in training and combat, I answered truthfully and everything was verified by Captain Garcia. In my service record I was entitled to: the Combat Infantry Badge, ETO medal with four battle stars, Bronze Star, Purple Heart, Good Conduct Medal, Victory in Europe Medal, and a Presidential Unit Citation.

When we left the office, the Lieutenant gave Garcia and me orders to pack our gear as we would be moving out by train to Plattsburg Barracks, New York. In Plattsburg, we would be checked out for any lingering combat disability and discharged honorably from there. Kramer would receive his honorable discharge from Camp Devers the following day, so Garcia and I wished him the best before leaving to board the train.

Arriving in Plattsburg at 0400 the following morning, Garcia and I were met at the station by a jeep driver who drove us to the barracks and helped with the baggage to our quarters. We were in the same building, but in different quarters. Sleeping until 1000 hours, I dressed, went downstairs, gave Garcia a wake-up call, and we reported to the main office with our service along with medical records, which we turned in.

Going to lunch in the main mess turned out to be fabulous lobster newburg, and that in itself was one hell of a big surprise in an army facility. After lunch we took a nap, then dressed and headed into town. In one of the hotels there was a nice bar and lounge called the "Fife and Drum," and that is where we met two very pretty French-Canadian girls from Montreal, Canada, only thirty miles away! As the night was young, we danced to the soft music filling this beautiful lounge, taking breaks at intervals to sip dry martinis. In about an hour we were joined by another Second Lieutenant in the Canadian Army, McCormack whom I had invited over to our table, along with his girl friend.

As the three couples continued downing the martinis, we began to feel more and more like all the world was a wonderful playground. One of the girls, Marie, spoke up, "everyone, let us do something daring and exciting! Let's go to New York City!" Then Captain Garcia said to McCormack and me, "Buzz, our commissions are temporary, we will be discharged soon, and any damn way, we don't have any duty for the weekend, so hopefully nobody will miss us before Monday! How about you, McCormack, are you free to go?" "You damn right matey's, being that I am in the same boat with you guys, I am free and meself won't be missed until Monday!" "Then let's get the hell out of here," I spoke up, "as the train from Montreal to New York arrives here in Plattsburg at midnight!"

Our party departed the Plattsburg Station at midnight and with several stopovers, including Albany and Newburgh, we arrived at New York's Grand Central Station at 0700 on Saturday morning. Upon stepping from the train and helping the ladies get their feet on solid ground, I had one hell of an embarrassing accident, the seat of my poplin suntan uniform pants split open. There wasn't anything I could do but hope to find a tailor as at present I was the favorite amusement of this happy party! After a short taxi ride from the station, the driver let the lot of us out close to the Empire State Building. Walking down toward this fabulous building, on a side street I saw a sign. "A. Lazarowitz, tailor." There was a coffee shop on the corner, so I said to the party, "you guys and gals have a cup of coffee because I am damn well going to get with this tailor, then I'll meet you here." When I entered the shop, an old Jewish gentleman asked, "Can I be of help to you, young officer?" "Yes, sir," I answered, "my uniform trousers are split all the way in the seat, and I would like to have a repair job!" "Wery vell," said the old tailor, "yust go in the booth, take off your pants and give to me them." I followed his instructions, and within five minutes he handed them back to me all stitched and repaired.. "Thank you, sir," I said, "how much do I owe you for this?" "Not vun penny, young officer," the old fellow answered, "I see from your ribbons that you fight in Europe, and maybe you helped liberate some of my people. I charge you nothing. Go with the Blessing of God!" "Thank you again Mr. Lazarowitz," I said as I departed the shop and joined my fine good-time friends at the coffee shop. "Three cheers for Buzz," said Garcia, as I joined them at the table, "He finally got his rear window fixed!" With that remark everyone had a big laugh as I modeled my newly repaired trousers for all to see!

As the group left the coffee shop and started walking toward the Empire State Building, just about all traffic had stopped on this wide street, even all pedestrians. Everyone was looking up toward the top of the fog and smoke shrouded building which showed a bright orange area near the top. This was the day that a B-26 bomber crashed into the Empire State Building, possibly due to the blanket of morning fog over New York City. The area had been declared off limits to all but emergency participants, so after looking for awhile, there was nothing we could do, so our group moved on feeling badly for those victims.

Our weekend party in New York City began as we set up headquarters in the Great Northern Hotel around the corner from Jack Dempsey's Restaurant. None of us had much money, but these three couples had one hell of a good time with what we had. Visiting many places of interest during daylight hours, the night life was enjoyed in many bars and night clubs along Broadway, and some Irish bars off the beaten path. In several Irish pubs the drinks were on the house or from an overloaded customer who was setting up the house. Our last two bars frequented on Saturday night were Diamond Jim's and Jack Dempsey's. Even in both of these bars, drinks were set up by anonymous donors for all three couples. What a friendly city to servicemen returning from V-E Day!

Leaving New York City at midnight Sunday, we arrived back in Plattsburg at 0500 Monday morning. McCormack and the three French-Canadian girls continued on to Montreal, while Garcia and I got off in Plattsburg. Garcia spoke up, "Buzz, since we have no passes, we better not go in the front gate to the barracks." "We don't have to go in the front gate, Garcia," I answered, "the railroad tracks pass right behind our building, so we follow the tracks, climb over the steel mesh fence and we'll be home free. I have already checked it out from my window." We then followed my directions exactly, and it damn well worked.

After a few hours sleep, Garcia and I made roll call and found out that neither of us had been missed the whole weekend. Here we were sneaking back, and worried about passes, when it wasn't even necessary. We could come and go as much as we wanted, so long as roll call was made each morning and no business was scheduled for the day.

Just about every evening the Steamboat Ticonderoga with a band and girls from the State Teacher's College in Plattsburg would make the run to Burlington, Vermont. Garcia and I were always present on that trip across Lake Champlain, and we enjoyed the food, drinks, and many pretty girls to dance with on the voyage. We also, most always escorted our dates home when the four-hour round trip was over. On one of these escapades, the girls were locked out so Garcia and I found a ladder, then escorted the two beauties to their upstairs bedrooms. When the family who owned the home returned in about an hour, Garcia and I made tracks down that ladder hardly touching a rung.

After a couple of weeks, Garcia was discharged honorably, and I was given a thirty-day furlough to go home, because my records had not yet been straightened out. We rode the train together to New York where Garcia would change for Texas and me for Virginia. On the way I met a very beautiful Irish lass "Pat" from Montreal, who was stopping off in Amsterdam, New York, to visit an aunt. She left the train in Poughkeepsie, where she gave me a nice farewell kiss, and her name, address, and phone number in Montreal, also an invitation to visit her home.

The parting in Grand Central Station with my best friend with whom I had been through hell was sad as we gave each other a farewell hug. With a promise to keep in touch, we disappeared from sight, as the darkness swallowed us up! Getting off the train in Fredericksburg, Virginia, I hitchhiked to my home, which I had not seen in two and one-half years. My mother and father were overwhelmed, as was my nephew, also the two pet dogs, at my arrival. I caught them totally surprised and it was wonderful.

After a nice dinner, I fired up my 1937 Pontiac Eight to visit my old girl friend who lived twenty miles away. The tires were very thin, so taking my nephew along was a good idea, as we had two flats before arriving at her home. She was overwhelmed also to see me and we enjoyed each other's company immensely. However, the war had left a mark on me, and due to no fault of hers, I realized that my feelings for her had changed. I was far too restless to even think of settling down in any way.

During this thirty-day furlough, my friend with whom I had known through the years arrived home from Europe, and suggested that we take a trip. This was right up my alley so driving to another state, we met and dated several very pretty girls during the week long trip. Two of these beauties came back to Richmond with us, and helped celebrate V-J Day, which had just occurred. Beer, Scotch and soda was flowing like water, as we celebrated the total end of this damn war, with the crowds of service people, as well as civilians who overran the streets of Richmond, Virginia.

After the celebration was over, we rested up, then saw the ladies off by train, before returning to our homes in the Virginia countryside. I did get to see many of my old friends during the rest of this furlough, but soon, too soon, it was time to return to Plattsburg.

Hitchhiking to Richmond, an automobile with two pretty sisters on their way to the city stopped and picked me up. Stopping at a road house, the three of us had quite a few beers. Leaving the joint, they drove me to the train station where I had already missed the train I was supposed to take. Since the next train was eight hours away the girls invited me to their apartment to rest until train time. I accepted, so the three of us had some more beer, then set on the side of a large bed which felt so comfortable that we stretched out across it and all three fell asleep. When I awoke, it was an hour until train time, so I washed up, left a note of thanks, then took a cab to the station. I didn't see these girls afterward, but really did appreciate their fine hospitality to a much lonely soldier with mixed feelings about what to do about his future.

Arriving back in Plattsburg, New York, I still had to wait two weeks before all of my records were straightened out. It was close to a weekend, so I went to Montreal, Canada, where getting together with my friend Lieutenant McCormack and two of the pretty French-Canadian ladies who accompanied us to New York, was really super. All had a great time sight-seeing, dancing, swimming, and what time was left we hit about every nightclub in Montreal. I did get to see the girl "Pat" (whom I had met earlier) on the train, Sunday evening before leaving Montreal.

Back in Plattsburg, I had some free time coming up so I decided to visit my brothers who were back from the war. First, I went to the U.S. Veteran's Hospital in Castle Point, New York, where my brother, "Joe," was recuperating from an injury he had received in North Africa, and we really enjoyed a nice two-day visit.

I then went by train from Castle Point to Boston where my brother, Lieutenant William G. Rice was now Personnel Officer at the Charlestown Naval Base there. He had recently returned from the South Pacific, where he had been attached to the Second Marine Division. When I reached the Naval Base, he was not on duty, so a naval Captain who knew "W.G." told me where he was living off base with his new wife. After getting lost several times along with taking the wrong subway, I finally found him at their apartment in the Brighton section of Boston. We had never seen a lot of each other as W.G. was a career Navy man, so this was a wonderful reunion. "Buzz," he said, "I am overwhelmed, and didn't even know you were back in the United States, also, I didn't know my little brother had a gold bar on his collar!" "This is only a temporary promotion, W.G., just to fill in an empty space created by an unforseeable occurrence," I answered, as we were called to lunch by "Skipper."

Staying at his place over the weekend, I departed on Monday morning for Plattsburg, riding on the train with an old Jewish gentleman who was going to Westfield, Massachusetts, after the Jewish holiday. This nice old fellow treated me with some of the best food and wine I had ever experienced.

Arriving back in Plattsburg, New York, where within a few days I received my honorable discharge, and returned home to Virginia. I could never get myself straight, no matter how hard I tried. For two years I went from job to job, but could not bring myself to settle down.

I knew that I had to find myself again, as the hell of war leaves a mark on many who experienced the horrors of it. In 1947, I joined the Merchant Marine, and my life follows in the book, "And the Sea Rolls on Forever."